The Curse Is Back . . .

The boy's swing crashed into the power lines almost silently.

But then a sharp crackling sound rose up over the screams of the riders and crowd down below.

A sharp crackling sound. A buzz. And a flash of yellow light.

Deirdre saw the boy's hands and feet fly up against the power lines.

The electricity sizzled around him.

His whole body twisted and jerked inside the buzzing yellow light.

And then the swing fell away, fell off the wires. Fell fast.

Deirdre knew when it landed. She could hear the sickening *crack*.

And then she shut her eyes and screamed and screamed and screamed.

Books by R. L. Stine

FEAR STREET
THE NEW GIRL
THE SURPRISE PARTY
THE OVERNIGHT
MISSING
THE WRONG NUMBER
THE SLEEPWALKER
HAUNTED
HALLOWEEN PARTY
THE STEPSISTER
SKI WEEKEND
THE FIRE GAME
LIGHTS OUT
THE SECRET BEDROOM
THE KNIFE
PROM QUEEN
FIRST DATE
THE BEST FRIEND
THE CHEATER
SUNBURN
THE NEW BOY
THE DARE
BAD DREAMS
DOUBLE DATE
THE THRILL CLUB
ONE EVIL SUMMER
THE MIND READER
WRONG NUMBER 2
TRUTH OR DARE
DEAD END
FINAL GRADE
SWITCHED
COLLEGE WEEKEND
THE STEPSISTER 2
WHAT HOLLY HEARD
THE FACE
SECRET ADMIRER
THE PERFECT DATE
THE CONFESSION
THE BOY NEXT DOOR

FEAR STREET SUPER CHILLERS
PARTY SUMMER
SILENT NIGHT
GOODNIGHT KISS
BROKEN HEARTS
SILENT NIGHT 2
THE DEAD LIFEGUARD
CHEERLEADERS: THE NEW EVIL
BAD MOONLIGHT
THE NEW YEAR'S PARTY
GOODNIGHT KISS 2

THE FEAR STREET SAGA
THE BETRAYAL
THE SECRET
THE BURNING

FEAR STREET CHEERLEADERS
THE FIRST EVIL
THE SECOND EVIL
THE THIRD EVIL

99 FEAR STREET: THE HOUSE OF EVIL
THE FIRST HORROR
THE SECOND HORROR
THE THIRD HORROR

THE CATALUNA CHRONICLES
THE EVIL MOON
THE DARK SECRET
THE DEADLY FIRE

FEAR STREET SAGAS
A NEW FEAR
HOUSE OF WHISPERS
FORBIDDEN SECRETS

FEAR PARK
THE FIRST SCREAM
THE LOUDEST SCREAM
THE LAST SCREAM

Available from **ARCHWAY** Paperbacks

FEAR STREET®
R·L·STINE

FEAR PARK #3

The Last Scream

A Parachute Press Book

AN ARCHWAY PAPERBACK
Published by POCKET BOOKS
New York London Toronto Sydney Tokyo Singapore

AN ARCHWAY PAPERBACK *Original*

An Archway Paperback published by
POCKET BOOKS, a division of Simon & Schuster Inc.
1230 Avenue of the Americas, New York, NY 10020

Copyright © 1996 by Parachute Press, Inc.

ISBN: 0-671-52957-9

First Archway Paperback printing October 1996

10 9 8 7 6 5 4 3 2 1

Cover art by Bill Schmidt

Printed in the U.S.A.

IL 7+

The Last Scream

chapter
1

Dierdre Bradley leaned forward on the hard bench. She wrapped her arms around herself to try to stop her shivers. With the cheers of the crowd buzzing in her ears, she stared down from the bleachers into the billowing purple smoke.

The teenagers on the field below raised hatchets over their shoulders and swung at the black tree stumps that dotted the ground. Soft music played, so soft Dierdre could barely hear it over the noise of the audience.

The purple smoke floated over the hardworking teenagers. It gave the scene an unreal quality. As the teenagers chopped at the stumps, swung, and chopped again, they all seemed to be moving in a dream.

It *is* a dream, Dierdre realized.

I'm asleep. And I'm dreaming that I'm in the bleachers, watching this show at Fear Park, at Daddy's park.

The Hatchet Show.

The reenactment of what really happened here sixty years ago.

The crowd cheered as, on the field below, two of the teenage actors broke into a shouting argument.

One boy roared with fury. Dierdre hugged herself tighter as he raised his hatchet. The blade gleamed purple, reflecting the eerie, billowing smoke.

The crowd cheered again as the boy swung the hatchet. And buried the blade deep in the other boy's chest.

The cheers of the audience turned to cries of horror as all of the teenagers furiously began to swing their hatchets at one another.

Chopping off arms. Slicing through backs and chests.

Hacking. Hacking at one another until the fake blood poured over the field, spreading like a thick, dark lake.

"Ohhhh." Dierdre heard herself utter a terrified moan.

The fake cries and wails of the teenage actors rose up over the cheers and applause of the audience.

Bodies sprawled in the spreading pool of blood. The music seemed to billow and swirl with the thick snakes of purple smoke.

This *really* happened, Dierdre thought, her teeth clenched, every muscle in her body tensed.

This really happened sixty years ago to teenagers working to clear the land for Fear Park. Without reason, they all went into a frenzy—dozens of them. And they chopped one another to pieces.

They all died. They all died on the spot where Daddy built his park sixty years later.

Their *real* blood soaked the ground where the teenagers put on their performances of the Hatchet Show today.

On the field below, the teenage actors swung and chopped away at one another. Dierdre closed her eyes to shut out the ugly scene.

But she couldn't get away from the cheers and laughter of the excited audience.

Why do they enjoy this show so much? she wondered. Why do they find it such a thrill to see kids butcher one another?

Why am I here watching it?

Because I'm dreaming.

She opened her eyes. And gazed down at the scene of horror.

"Huh?" Dierdre gasped as a dark-haired boy stepped out from a thick swirl of purple smoke. She sat high in the bleachers. But she recognized him at once.

"Robin!"

Robin Fear. Her friend. Her closest friend.

More than her friend. Her boyfriend. Her *protector*.

"Robin—what are you doing there? Get *away* from there!" she called to him.

Of course he couldn't hear her. His dark eyes scanned the crowd, as if searching for her.

"Robin! Robin!" Dierdre screamed. "Robin—please! Get away!"

He pulled a long-handled hatchet out of his shoulder.

Behind him, two boys chopped at each other's legs.

They both collapsed to the ground—and on their torn, bleeding knees continued chopping and hacking at each other's chests.

Wails of horror and pain rose up through the music, through the clouds of purple smoke.

Robin turned to the frenzied teenagers. Dierdre watched him hoist back his hatchet and prepare to swing.

"No! No—please!" she begged.

Why is Robin doing that? Why is Robin on the field? Why is Robin in the Hatchet Show?

"Please—Robin! Get away!"

And then she thought: Why am I screaming? This is a dream.

I only need to wake up.

Wake up, Dierdre, she urged herself. *Wake up. Wake up.*

She waited for that feeling of release, that rising feeling when you feel yourself pulling up out of a dream.

Wake up, Dierdre. Come on—wake up.

She blinked, expecting to find herself in her room. Safe in bed.

But the wails of pain continued, rising over the cheers and applause of the crowd. The audience was on its feet now, standing and clapping in rhythm with the swings of the gleaming hatchets.

It's a dream. Only a dream, Dierdre assured herself.

But no matter how hard she tried, she couldn't pull herself out of it.

She blinked hard. Shut her eyes, waited, then opened them again.

4

Still there. All the horror, the blood, the pain—still there.

It's not a dream, Dierdre realized.

I'm awake. I'm not dreaming.

Bodies and parts of bodies lay strewn across the field. A few kids remained standing, swinging and hacking at one another wearily.

Robin swung his hatchet wildly, back and forth in a wide half circle.

All real, Dierdre thought, shivering in horror.

All real. It's happening again.

I'm awake. And it's happening again.

"Robin! Robin—look out!"

chapter
2

C *hop. Chop. Chop.*

The teenagers attacked one another like machines now, in a deliberate, steady rhythm.

The ugly hacking sounds sent cold shudders down Dierdre's back. She shut her eyes again.

When she opened them, she sat in her room. At her desk.

Wide awake.

Afternoon sunlight streamed in through the open bedroom window. A soft breeze fluttered the white curtains.

"Oh." She swallowed hard. She struggled to catch her breath. Her stomach churned. She still hugged herself tightly.

"I wasn't asleep," she murmured out loud. Her eyes focused on the bulletin board on the lemon-colored wall above her desk. She searched for the date on the calendar posted there. She needed to find something real. Something . . . ordinary.

She grabbed the red and blue Koosh ball she kept on the desk beside her computer, and squeezed it tightly in one hand.

It wasn't a dream, she realized.

I was awake the whole time.

So what was it?

A vision, she decided. Some kind of vision—of the future?

A peek at a horror to come?

Dierdre sighed. Fear Park had been struck by so many horrors. So many people had died. Hideous deaths. Unexplained deaths.

Before the park even opened, the manager of the animal preserve had been mauled to death and eaten by the lions he had gone to feed.

A bomb had exploded in the House of Mirrors, sending sharp chunks of glass flying, killing twelve people.

Dierdre's boyfriend Paul had somehow gotten trapped beneath the Ferris wheel. The wheel beheaded him and crushed his body.

As Dierdre watched in shock and disbelief, Paul's brother, Jared, and three of his friends had their bodies ripped apart by a mysterious force.

So many deaths. So much horror.

So much horror that Dierdre was beginning to believe the rumors that a curse had been placed on Fear Park. She never wanted to believe any of it. Even when her father talked about the curse, Dierdre chose to ignore it.

After all, this was nearly the twenty-first century.

Why would anyone believe in ancient curses today?

Dierdre shook her head sadly. It was hard to know *what* to believe.

The park had begun in horror. Why did those teenagers helping to clear the land for the park in 1935 go wild and hack one another to death?

It had never been explained.

And now Dierdre had seen some kind of vision. A warning about the future. A warning that the frenzied killing could take place once again.

Dad has to close the park forever, she told herself. He has to forget his dream. He has to close the park and walk away—before more innocent people die. Before more blood darkens the ground where it was built.

The park had been closed for a month while police investigated the last deaths that occurred. And while workers made a safety check on every part of the park.

But Dierdre's dad, Jason Bradley, was determined to open again as soon as the city would allow.

He can't, Dierdre decided. Fear Park should never open its gates again.

Dierdre climbed unsteadily to her feet. She decided to go downstairs and force her dad to listen to her. As she made her way to the bedroom door, she felt shaky and weak.

That vision exhausted me, she realized.

She held on tightly to the banister as she walked down the stairs. "Dad? Hey, Dad?"

No reply.

She checked the small kitchen. Checked the living room. Then peeked into his room.

"Dad?"

Did he go out?

A muffled groan caught her attention.

The bathroom door swung open. Mr. Bradley lurched out into his bedroom bare-chested, shaving cream on his face. His eyes bulged wide with alarm, and he uttered a hoarse choking sound.

"Dad!" Dierdre gasped.

"Unnnnnh!"

He grabbed his throat. His eyes bulged even wider.

"Dad—what's wrong? Are you choking?" Dierdre cried.

He nodded frantically. Then with another choked groan he opened his mouth wide and jammed his fingers down his throat.

"Unnnnh. Unnnnnnh."

Dierdre froze. What should she do? "Dad—should I call for help? Call 911?"

"Unnnnh."

He struggled with his hand in his mouth. Probing deep into his throat with his fingers.

"Aaaaagh!"

He let out a cry as he finally tugged his fingers out.

Dierdre screamed when she saw what he had pulled from his throat.

A long, fat brown worm wriggled between his fingers.

Dierdre gagged, sickened at the sight.

"Ohhhh." Mr. Bradley uttered a weak moan.

"How—" Dierdre started to ask.

But she couldn't finish her question. Her father started to choke again.

He probed his fingers into this throat, his eyes rolling wildly. Shaving cream smeared over his hands, his trousers, the wall.

With a horrified gasp he pulled another long worm from deep in his throat. He held it in front of his face, watched it quiver between his fingers, then dropped it to the floor.

Mr. Bradley's chin trembled. His entire body shook. He choked again.

"Daddy!" Dierdre shrieked.

She watched him pull an even longer worm from his mouth. Then two more. Then two more.

He let the worms fall to the floor. Dierdre saw them crawling over his bare feet.

"H-help!" Mr. Bradley finally managed to whisper.

But what could Dierdre do?

She watched as he pulled another fat, foot-long worm off his tongue.

What is going on? she wondered. What is *happening* here?

chapter 3

Robin Fear snickered to himself and passed his hand once more over the steaming silver bowl. Candlelight flickered across the floor of the small library, casting darting shadows over the walls of old books.

A pleased smile crossed Robin's usually somber face. This dark library was his favorite place. It had been his father's favorite place too. All of the ancient books about sorcery, magic, and the dark arts had belonged to his father.

They were Robin's now. And he knew how to use them.

He knew how to use magic to get what he wanted—*whatever* he wanted.

He had used the powers of the old books to make himself and Meghan Fairwood immortal. Robin and Meghan were born in 1918. That meant they were nearly eighty years old.

Eighty years old and still teenagers. For Robin had frozen their ages at seventeen. That meant they would stay seventeen forever and never age a day.

He passed his hand once again over the bowl of steaming black liquid. He chanted the ancient words softly to himself.

Yes. The old books gave Robin power. The power to get whatever he wanted. The power to *do* whatever he wanted.

Right now he was amusing himself by making worms appear in Jason Bradley's throat.

Simple. But funny.

One of the simplest spells of all. It helped Robin relax.

He had a lot to be tense about. Because the ancient magic he knew hadn't brought him what he wanted most in the world.

He wanted to destroy Fear Park. He *needed* to destroy Fear Park. To close it down and make sure it stayed closed forever.

With a sigh, Robin thought back on the long and tragic history of Fear Park. . . .

In 1935 Nicholas Fear, Robin's father, vowed that the park would never go up. The Bradley family wanted to build their amusement park in a section of the Fear Street Woods. Nicholas Fear was determined to keep the land for the Fear family.

The town of Shadyside voted to allow the park to be built. But Robin's father swore to do everything he could to stop it.

Robin promised to help his father. After the land had been cleared by the Bradleys, a group of teenagers was hired to clear the tree stumps. Robin cast the spell that made the teenagers go wild and hack one another to death.

After Nicholas Fear died, Robin continued the battle to keep the Bradleys from opening the park. But the Bradley family proved more stubborn than Robin had imagined.

Sixty years later, Fear Park was ready to open its gates. Robin continued to plot and scheme. He got a job at the park running the Ferris wheel. He became close with Jason Bradley's daughter, Dierdre. Robin made Dierdre fall in love with him. He convinced her that she could always confide in him, trust him.

And all the while he plotted against Dierdre and her father.

So far Robin had caused a lot of death and destruction. But he had failed—Fear Park was about to open again in a few days.

The Bradleys would triumph over the Fears after all. Unless Robin acted quickly.

Lost in his unhappy thoughts, Robin swept his hand over the steaming bowl, sending another fat brown worm to Jason Bradley's throat.

"Robin—there you are!" a voice called. "What are you doing?"

Robin raised his eyes to see Meghan burst into the library. Her long, wavy red hair swept behind her. She glanced around the small room, her green eyes reflecting the shimmering candlelight.

Robin held his hand over the steaming bowl. Across town, Jason Bradley would start to choke on another fat worm.

"What are you doing?" Meghan asked again, standing over him. He could smell the sweet orangy fragrance of her perfume.

"It's a protection spell," Robin lied.

Meghan furrowed her brow. "Protection?"

Robin nodded. "The Bradleys are opening Fear Park again tomorrow. I've been searching and searching through Father's old books. Looking for a spell to protect them from any more tragedies. I think I may have found one."

Kneeling on the floor, he gazed up at her and studied her face. Does she believe me? he asked himself. Is she buying that story?

He couldn't tell. She shut her eyes and let out a long, weary sigh.

Robin climbed to his feet and moved to her. "What's wrong?" he demanded.

"I don't know," she replied, shaking her head. "I'm just so tired."

"Tired? Of what?"

"Of everything." She sighed. She pushed a strand of coppery hair off her forehead. "I'm tired of you spending all of your time worrying about the Bradleys. I've seen you with that Bradley girl, Robin, and I—"

"I explained that," Robin interrupted. He put his hands on the shoulders of her green sweater and held her, as if to calm her.

"You know why I spend all my time worrying about the Bradleys," he said softly, peering into her eyes. "I—I feel so guilty. My father put a curse on them.

He put a curse on their park. And I've tried so hard to lift the curse."

He squeezed her shoulders, holding her in place. He stared intently into her eyes as if hypnotizing her. She lowered her gaze to the rows of candles on the floor.

"So many innocent people have died because of my father," Robin said in a trembling voice. "I feel responsible, Meghan. I feel that I have to do everything I can to make sure that more innocent people don't die in Fear Park."

Is she buying it? he wondered. She has believed my lies for sixty years. Is she buying them now?

She sighed again. "I guess I'm just tired of everything," she whispered. "I'm tired of being immortal. Tired of being seventeen for my whole life."

She raised pleading eyes to him. "I don't want to stay like this, Robin. I know what you're doing is good. I know how much it means to you. But I don't want to stay here in this young body. I want to grow old. I don't want to live in a time we don't belong in."

I'm tired too, Robin thought bitterly.

Tired of listening to Meghan complain. I made her immortal. I brought her with me because I loved her, because I cared about her so much. Because I needed to have her with me.

But she has never been happy. She has complained the whole time. And she has become more and more bitter as the years have passed.

Robin stood holding on to her shoulders, staring into her green eyes. I cared about her so much, he thought. I needed her so much.

But I don't need her now.

And I don't even *like* her that much.

She's tired of being seventeen. And I'm tired of her.

"Do you understand what I'm telling you?" Meghan asked. "Do you understand why I can't go on like this?"

"Yes," he replied softly. "Yes. And I will help you, Meghan."

Slowly he slid his hands off her shoulders and wrapped them around her throat.

Then, still staring deep into her eyes, he began to squeeze.

chapter
4

Of course, she is immortal, Robin reminded himself. I cannot strangle her. She cannot die.

He loosened his grip on her throat.

Meghan smiled at him.

She thinks I was being tender, he realized. She has no idea of what I really intended to do.

He leaned forward and kissed her forehead, a quick peck.

"Do you really mean it?" Meghan asked, pressing her forehead against his shoulder.

He nodded. "When I'm sure the park is safe," he told her. "When I'm sure the Bradleys are safe from my father's curse, I will find a spell. I promise. I will find a way for you and me to grow old together."

"Oh, thank you, Robin!" she cried. She threw her arms around him and kissed him gratefully.

The kiss tasted sour on Robin's lips.

Maybe there *is* a spell that will rid me of her, he

17

thought. I'll be much happier without Meghan around.

At least she still believes me, still trusts me, he thought, returning her kiss.

But I no longer need her. I'll find a way to kill her—after I destroy Fear Park forever.

Dierdre Bradley's skin prickled. She used a wadded-up tissue to mop sweat from her forehead.

It was a cool, clear evening. But the trailer that served as Jason Bradley's office radiated with heat.

Dierdre groaned and rolled her eyes. "Daddy, what is your problem? It's a beautiful night. Why do you have all the windows closed?"

Without waiting for an answer, she crossed the narrow trailer and slid up one of the square windows.

"I don't know," her father murmured. "I guess I feel safer with them closed."

"You've *got* to breathe," Dierdre scolded.

"Don't know if I'll ever feel safe again," Mr. Bradley whispered, lowering his eyes.

The ugly, fat worms must have damaged his vocal cords, Dierdre realized. He can't speak louder than a whisper. She had urged him to go see Dr. Kleinsmith at Shadyside General immediately. But he stubbornly refused. He didn't like doctors.

Besides, Dierdre believed he was embarrassed.

How could he ever explain to a doctor that he had pulled out nearly a dozen foot-long worms from his mouth?

Dierdre shuddered and tried to force the slimy brown creatures out of her mind.

That was yesterday.

This was a new day. A Friday night. The grand reopening of Fear Park.

As the sun lowered behind the trees, people started to arrive. By dark the park was crowded.

Cheerful voices and children's laughter floated into the trailer office through the open window. Dierdre gazed at her father. He didn't seem to hear the voices. He seemed to be off in another world, a world of his own unhappy thoughts.

She stepped up behind his chair and rested her hands on his shoulders. He had always been a big, powerful man. Bearlike. But he seemed smaller to Dierdre now. Weaker. As if all the problems and tragedies had shrunk him.

"Dad—are you okay?" she asked.

He didn't reply.

I really can't bear to see him like this, Dierdre thought unhappily.

"The gates opened an hour ago," she told him. "And the park is already crowded." She squeezed his shoulders. "Doesn't that make you feel good?"

"Not really," he murmured in his hoarse, strained voice.

He swiveled his chair around to face her. He stared up at her with red-rimmed eyes. "I've been thinking a lot about our discussion last night," he whispered.

"Dad, I'm sorry—"

Dierdre and her father had talked long into the night. She begged and argued and pleaded for her dad not to reopen Fear Park.

Now Dierdre felt guilty about some of the things

she had said. Her words had obviously hurt her father.

And her pleading had been in vain. Jason had completely refused to listen to her. There was no way he would even think about keeping the park closed.

She had ended up screaming at him and storming out of the room. She felt childish and guilty even though she strongly believed she was right.

The park was cursed. Why couldn't her father see that?

Why did he have to be so stubborn? Hadn't enough innocent people died?

"Do you want to be responsible for even more deaths?" she had shrieked at him the night before.

Jason Bradley's face turned beet red.

Dierdre knew she had gone too far.

But why wouldn't he listen?

Now he stared up at her from his wooden desk chair, his face lined, his eyes so red and tired. "I owe you more of an explanation," he said softly. His eyes watered, and he lowered his gaze to the floor.

"Daddy, we said it all last night." Dierdre sighed, turning to the window.

"No," he protested. "We didn't say it all. At least, I didn't."

A heavy silence hung inside the stuffy trailer. Dierdre crossed her arms in front of her. A wisp of her dark brown hair fell over one eye. But she didn't move to brush it away.

Bouncy calliope music from the carousel floated in through the window. Dierdre could hear the rattle of rifle fire from the shooting gallery across the midway.

"There is a lot you don't know, Dierdre," Mr. Bradley said finally. He cleared his throat painfully, and gently rubbed his neck. "There is a lot I haven't told you."

Dierdre lowered herself to the edge of the desk. Her legs suddenly felt weak. Her heart thudded.

What was he about to say?

"Sure, this park is my dream," Mr. Bradley continued. "It was my father's dream. And his father's dream. And I made it my goal in life. That's one reason I've been so stubborn about keeping the park open."

"I know, Daddy," Dierdre replied. "We've already said—"

"But that isn't the only reason," Jason Bradley continued. "You see, I—I—"

He hesitated. Rubbed his stubbly jaw. "This is hard for me, Dierdre. But I might as well just get it out."

He narrowed his eyes at her. "You see, I've put every penny into this park. Every penny. If the park goes under, we don't have enough money to buy a hot dog."

Dierdre gasped. Her mouth dropped open. The walls of the small trailer appeared to close in on her.

"But what about the savings account, Dad? All the money Mom left you when she died?"

Mr. Bradley avoided Dierdre's gaze. "I . . . I sank it into the park," he said so low she could barely hear him. "I cleared out the bank account and invested it in the park. That money hasn't been there for at least two years."

Dierdre swallowed hard. "We're really broke?"

21

Mr. Bradley nodded. He shut his eyes. "We're worse than broke. I had to take out some personal loans to keep us going. Several loans, I'm afraid. The investors refused to put in any more money. They said the park was doomed. They wanted me to buy them out. I—I—" He gazed up guiltily at Dierdre.

"So you put in our own money," Dierdre said grimly.

"And borrowed more." A sob escaped Mr. Bradley. He covered his mouth, pretending it was a hiccup.

The *tat-tat-tat-tat* of rifle shot from the arcade drummed in Dierdre's ears. She gritted her teeth, trying to shut out the noise, trying to concentrate on her father's startling words.

She realized she had been holding her breath. She let it out in a loud *whoosh*.

"I haven't told you the worst part," Jason Bradley murmured, his eyes glistening. He ran a hand heavily back over his bushy hair. Then he cleared his aching throat again.

"There's more?" Dierdre asked weakly.

"Your college account," Mr. Bradley whispered.

"Oh, no!" Dierdre blurted out. "You *didn't!* The money Mom left me for college?"

With a groan Mr. Bradley climbed to his feet. He crossed the small trailer and hugged Dierdre. "I'm sorry. Really, Dee. I'm so sorry."

"All of it?" Dierdre choked out.

"I'm afraid so," her father replied, holding on to her. "I'm afraid so. All of it. All of your money. I had no choice. I had to use it for the park."

"So we really don't have any money to live on?" Dierdre asked. "No money at all?"

Mr. Bradley let go of Dierdre and stepped to the trailer door. "No. No money," he whispered. "Unless Fear Park is a success."

Dierdre swallowed again. Her hands suddenly felt ice cold. She tucked them into her jeans pockets.

She took a deep breath. "Then we have no choice," she said, forcing herself to sound hopeful. "We have to make Fear Park a big success."

Dierdre forced a smile. This smile, she thought, is the bravest thing I've ever done.

"We've got to make Fear Park the biggest and most popular amusement park in the world!" she declared, struggling to sound cheerful, struggling to sound as if she meant it.

"Yes," Mr. Bradley agreed in a whisper. "Yes. Yes. And we have to make sure that nothing else goes wrong. Nothing. No more deaths. No more accidents."

"Everything will go right from now on!" Dierdre proclaimed. "I know it will, Daddy. I know it will."

They both jumped when they heard the sound.

A girl's cry outside the trailer.

A high, shrill scream of horror.

chapter
5

Dierdre lurched to the trailer window. She leaned over and stuck her head out.

She squinted into the bright lights of the front walkway—and saw Robin Fear. He was walking quickly, crossing in front of a group of little kids, heading toward the trailer.

Another shrill scream made Dierdre turn her head to the right. She glimpsed two teenage boys carrying a girl on their shoulders. She was screaming and pretending to struggle as they threatened to toss her in the big fountain.

They lowered her toward the high spray of colored water. And she screamed again.

"What is it, Dee? What's wrong?" Mr. Bradley called from behind her, his thin voice quaking with alarm.

Dierdre pulled her head back into the trailer and

turned to him. "No problem. Just some kids having fun. Messing around."

"I thought—" Mr. Bradley started to say. His face was bright red. His chest heaved up and down beneath his Hawaiian sport shirt.

"It's okay. Really, Daddy," Dierdre assured him. "Two boys are teasing a girl. She—"

Dierdre stopped as the trailer door swung open. She turned to the front as Robin leaned in.

"Hi. Aren't you working tonight?" she greeted him.

"Yes. My shift at the Ferris wheel starts in ten minutes," Robin replied, glancing at his watch. "I just wanted to stop by and see how it was going. You know. Wish you good luck."

"That's very nice of you, Rob," Mr. Bradley said.

"Everything is fine," Dierdre told him. "Daddy and I were just talking about the park. We're going to make it the most popular amusement park in the world!"

"Really?" Robin stared at Dierdre, then at her father. He had been smiling. But the smile faded quickly.

Dierdre could see how much her words had surprised Robin. A few days before, she had promised Robin that she would talk to her father. She promised she would convince her father to close the park—and keep it closed.

"We don't want any more innocent lives lost," Robin had said.

And Dierdre agreed.

But now, here she was, forcing herself to sound

cheerful. Bragging about how wonderful and successful the park was going to be.

Robin is definitely confused, Dierdre saw. That's because he doesn't know the whole story. He doesn't know what terrible trouble Dad and I will be in if the park fails.

"I'll explain everything to Robin later, she decided. She knew he'd understand. He was the kindest, most understanding boy she'd ever met.

"Well, good luck!" Robin declared. He raised two fingers to his forehead and gave Dierdre a quick salute. "Meet me later? My shift is over at ten."

"Okay. See you later," Dierdre agreed.

The trailer door closed behind him. Dierdre moved to the window and watched Robin make his way through the crowd to the Ferris wheel.

A sharp cry made Dierdre turn her attention to a little red-haired girl chasing a red balloon across the pathway. A long string trailed beneath the balloon. But the wind was carrying the balloon up, just out of the girl's reach.

The little girl cried out as she tripped and went sprawling facedown on the pavement. She remained on the ground for a few moments, arms and legs twisted—which made Dierdre's heart stop.

But by the time the parents came running over, the girl was back on her feet, rubbing her knee and pointing to the escaped balloon.

Dierdre breathed a long sigh of relief. "I hope a skinned knee is the worst thing that happens tonight," she murmured.

"What?" her father called.

She turned to find him seated at the small, cluttered desk. His face was lowered over a stack of papers, which he shuffled through quickly.

"Nothing," Dierdre told him. "Just talking to myself."

The phone rang. Mr. Bradley reached for it, but Dierdre picked it up first. "Hello?"

"You don't know Robin," a voice rasped.

"Excuse me?" Dierdre cried. She pulled the receiver from her ear and stared at it as if there were something wrong with it.

"You don't know the truth about Robin," the voice whispered. *"You'd better find out about him. Before it's too late."*

"Who is this?" Dierdre demanded angrily. "Why do you keep calling me? Why are you *doing* this?"

chapter
6

Robin kicked a soda can across the path. It bounced off the sneaker of a boy up ahead. The boy didn't seem to notice.

Scowling, leaning into the gusting wind, Robin had his fists stuffed into his jeans pockets. To keep himself from punching someone. Anyone.

He pictured himself landing a sharp punch on Dierdre's jaw. Pictured her shocked expression as she sank to the ground, her pretty face swelling. Ruined. Her teeth scattered at her feet.

Control your anger, he warned himself.

It wasn't easy. He hadn't felt this angry in a lot of years.

But why shouldn't I be angry at Dierdre? he asked himself. She betrayed me. She's a liar. And a traitor.

Robin had worked so hard to convince Dierdre that Fear Park should never reopen. She had promised to force her father to give up the park.

But now here she was, bragging about how Fear Park was going to be such a big success.

How many people do I have to kill to convince Dierdre that the park has to close? Robin thought bitterly.

He answered his own question: just one.

Robin had been planning to kill Dierdre. He figured that losing his daughter might convince Jason Bradley that the park was cursed. Might convince the man to pack up and go away.

But Bradley is so stubborn, Robin decided. He's so stubborn that even losing Dierdre might not force him to close the park.

That left Robin no choice. He had to kill Jason Bradley.

I should have done it long ago, Robin scolded himself. Why didn't I think of it first?

Fear Park is Jason Bradley's dream. And it is a dream that will die with him.

I guess I wanted to make Mr. Bradley suffer first, Robin decided as he stepped up to the control panel to the Ferris wheel. I wanted Dierdre's dad to see all the tragedy his park caused, all the lives lost.

But I can't wait any longer.

Besides, poor Mr. Bradley has suffered enough. It's time to put him out of his misery.

Robin waved to Ronnie Scott, Ferris wheel operator for the early shift. Ronnie grinned and stuck his green bubble gum through his teeth.

Robin had a strong urge to knock the gum down Ronnie's throat. Instead, he murmured, "How's it going?"

He didn't listen to Ronnie's answer. He was thinking about Jason Bradley. Watching the Ferris wheel spin. And thinking about Jason Bradley.

"See ya," he heard Ronnie say. The lanky young man strode away, brushing his short blond hair back with both hands.

Robin reached for the lever that controlled the wheel. The ride was full, he saw. The little cars rolled down, then, with a gentle tilt, swung back up again, all of them filled.

Robin watched for a long while. Thinking hard.

He saw two teenage boys riding with their hands straight up in the air, as if they were on a wild roller-coaster ride. A car with two girls passed by. The girls were leaning forward, making the car rock.

A white-haired couple shared the next car. They held hands and had their heads tilted back in laughter. In the next car, a boy and girl were kissing, their arms wrapped around each other.

Cute, Robin thought bitterly. Real cute.

Seeing people have a good time filled him with disgust.

He knew it was time to unload passengers. And load new passengers on. The line of people waiting for the Ferris wheel stretched out onto the pathway. Some people were starting to appear impatient.

But Robin wasn't ready to stop the wheel. He had a better idea.

He grabbed the heavy steel lever. And, snickering to himself, he shoved it forward—all the way.

The big wheel hesitated at first. Then Robin heard

some of the passengers squeal as it jerked them hard—and quickly picked up speed.

The cars all rocked and tilted as the wheel began to spin faster. The lights on the wheel frame blended into a single circle of light.

Faster.

Squeals turned to screams.

From down on the ground Robin heard gasps of shock. The people waiting in line began to point and cry out in surprise.

Faster.

The white-haired couple were no longer holding hands. Their hands were gripped tightly around the safety bar as their car swung and lurched. The two boys continued riding with their hands up in the air. The boys whooped loudly, laughing, enjoying the wild ride.

The two girls who had been leaning forward . . .

Robin couldn't see what the two girls were doing. The big wheel was whirling too fast now to see any of the passengers clearly. They had all become a blur of color. A rippling wash of wide eyes and frightened faces.

The screams and squeals rose over the loud clack of the Ferris wheel, over the alarmed cries of everyone watching from the ground.

Robin leaned into the heavy steel lever, as if trying to push it even farther.

"Stop it! Stop it!" someone screamed from nearby.

"My little girl is up there!"

"Oh, no! Noooooo!"

"Somebody—do something!"

Robin couldn't help it. He tossed back his head and laughed.

But he cut the laugh short when he saw two Fear Park security guards shoving their way through the crowd, running toward him. "What's wrong?" one of them called breathlessly.

"Stop that thing!" his partner demanded.

"I—I can't!" Robin cried, forcing fear to his face, making his hands tremble on the lever. "It's stuck!"

"Huh?" Both guards uttered startled cries.

"The lever is stuck!" Robin told them. "I can't budge it!"

A loud shriek from the whirring wheel made Robin and the two guards turn. A large glob of green appeared to fly off the wheel. It flew through the air and splattered over the crowd of onlookers.

Cries of disgust rose up over the shrill shrieks of the spinning passengers. Another glob of green came flying from the wheel and splattered onto a man's head and shoulders.

It took Robin a few seconds to realize what the green globs were. One of the Ferris wheel passengers was vomiting.

"Do something!"

"Stop it! Can't somebody stop it?"

The cries sounded more shrill, more panicky.

"Let me try to pull the lever back," one of the security guards demanded, starting to push Robin out of the way.

"No!" Robin protested. "Go get Mr. Bradley. He'll know what to do."

The two guards hesitated.

"Go get Mr. Bradley!" Robin screamed. "Hurry!"

They turned and ran, their brown and gold uniform jackets flying behind them.

Robin watched them push through the horrified crowd. Then he turned back to enjoy the whirring Ferris wheel.

It had grown quieter on the wheel, he noticed. Fewer passengers were screaming.

Did they realize that it didn't help them to scream? Or had some of them passed out?

The wheel whipped around too rapidly for Robin to see. He could make out the blurred forms of people being tossed back and forth inside the cars.

The gears of the big wheel made a deafening grinding sound. A roar of metal against metal. The cars squeaked and squealed as they rocked up, then down.

"What is the problem?"

Robin spun around to see Mr. Bradley trotting toward him, flanked by the two security guards. His face was red, and his mouth hung open in a broad O of horror.

"Robin—stop that thing!"

"I can't!" Robin insisted. He pretended to tug on the lever.

"My son is on that thing!" a woman screamed.

"Why aren't you stopping it?" another woman cried angrily. Others jammed forward, shouting and furiously asking questions.

The two guards forced the crowd away, trying to calm them.

Here's my chance, Robin decided.

Mr. Bradley stepped up to the lever. "Move over, Rob. Let me try it," he said, reaching for it.

Robin stepped in the way. "No. You can't," he said softly.

"Huh?" Mr. Bradley's features twisted in bewilderment. "Move aside," he ordered sharply. "Let me try it."

"You can't," Robin repeated firmly.

"Why not?" Mr. Bradley demanded.

"Because you're dead," Robin told him.

34

chapter
7

Mr. Bradley stared at Robin in total confusion.

Robin tried to force it back—but a grin spread quickly over his mouth.

"What did you say?" Mr. Bradley demanded.

"You're dead," Robin repeated calmly.

Mr. Bradley let out an angry growl. He grabbed for the lever. "Give me that!"

Robin let go of the lever. He lowered his shoulder— and rammed hard into Mr. Bradley's chest.

"Unh!" Mr. Bradley uttered a startled grunt. He staggered back, off balance.

Robin drove another shoulder block into Jason Bradley's midsection.

The big man let out a startled moan as he toppled backward.

Into the whirring, squealing wheel.

A metal car swung up—and caught Mr. Bradley on the back of the head.

The sound of the *crack* was so loud, it drowned out the startled gasps all around.

The metal footrest of the car caught the back of Mr. Bradley's skull and lifted him off the ground. Then, as the car swung higher, he dropped off, crumpling in a broken heap on the pavement.

A puddle of bright blood spread under his head.

His eyes were opened wide, staring up blankly at Robin. One leg was twisted at an impossible angle beneath his broad body.

He didn't move.

Cries and shrieks made Robin cover his ears. He forced the grin off his face.

"Mr. Bradley," he said out loud, "you're history."

And so is Fear Park, Robin thought happily.

"Daddy! Daddy!"

The shrill cry interrupted Robin's happy thoughts.

He turned to see Dierdre, her face twisted in horror. She dropped onto her knees beside her father. "Daddy! Daddy!"

A sob escaped her throat. She turned to Robin. "What happened?"

"The lever is jammed," Robin replied, kneeling beside her. "I couldn't move it. Your dad—he tried to help me. But he slipped. He—he hit his head."

"Oh, no. Noooooooooo," Dierdre wailed, raising her hands to her cheeks. "Noooooo."

"I tried to catch him," Robin said. "But he slipped out of my hands. A car swung up and—"

"We need an ambulance!" Dierdre shrieked, jumping to her feet. "Somebody—call an ambulance."

"Dierdre—" Robin started to say. But she didn't hear him.

"I'll do it myself!" She took off, hurtling through the crowd toward the office trailer.

Robin turned his gaze to her father. Mr. Bradley groaned and blinked his eyes.

"No!" Robin gasped. *He's alive. He's still alive. No. That can't be. No. No way. No way.*

Robin dropped to his knees, wrapped his hands around Jason Bradley's throat, and started to strangle him.

chapter 8

Robin glanced up—and realized too many people were watching. A tight circle of onlookers stared down at him, murmuring to one another, shaking their heads, faces pale with alarm.

He hesitated.

I can't let him live. I *can't*.

But what can I do?

Before he could decide, Robin heard a familiar voice calling his name. A second later Meghan dropped down beside him.

She gasped in horror. "Robin—what are you *doing?*"

"Meghan—what are *you* doing here?" he demanded.

She ignored his question, gaping at him in wide-eyed confusion.

Robin gazed down at his hands, still wrapped around Mr. Bradley's throat.

"I—uh—I'm trying to revive him," he told Meghan.

Mr. Bradley's eyes were shut now. His breaths came in sharp wheezes. His hair was matted in dark blood.

Robin removed his hands from the man's throat. He turned to Meghan. "It's Mr. Bradley," he explained. "He had a bad accident. But he's still alive. I thought if I could get him to open his eyes . . ."

"Robin—you'd better leave him be," Meghan warned. She put a hand on Robin's arm and tried to tug him away.

Robin heard the high wail of a siren in the distance. The ambulance is on the way, he realized.

Please have a flat tire! he said silently to himself.

Please give Mr. Bradley a chance to die.

Jason Bradley's chest rose and fell with each wheezing breath.

Robin allowed Meghan to pull him to the side. "You're just too good," she whispered in his ear.

"What?"

"You think you can save everyone," Meghan said, holding on to his arm, pressing her cheek against his.

The orangy smell of her perfume disgusted him.

I used to love her, he thought. Now I have no feeling at all for her.

What is she saying?

"You're not a doctor," Meghan continued heatedly. "You think you can save the Bradleys. You think you can save everyone. You've worked so hard all these years trying to protect them."

She stared into Robin's eyes. "But you can't do

39

everything, Robin. You can't save the world. You're just too good. Too good." She kissed his cheek.

A smile broke over Robin's face. He turned away so that Meghan couldn't see it.

Yes. That's my problem, he thought bitterly. I'm just *too good*.

I've been with Meghan for over sixty years. And I never realized till this moment just how stupid she is!

Robin pulled Meghan aside as white-uniformed medics swarmed toward the Ferris wheel. One of them managed to stop the wheel. Two ambulances made their way slowly through the crowd. "If he dies, do you think the park will close?" Meghan asked.

"Probably," Robin replied. He saw Dierdre on her knees beside the medics. Her brown hair had fallen over her tearstained face. Her whole body trembled as she watched the medics work.

A few minutes later he saw Dierdre climb into the back of the ambulance, followed by the stretcher carrying Mr. Bradley.

He suddenly felt weary. Weary and disappointed.

What if Mr. Bradley lives?

What then?

"Let's go home," he told Meghan. "They found someone to unload the passengers. And no one is going to want to ride the Ferris wheel now. They won't need me any more tonight."

"Don't worry, Robin," Meghan said softly. Holding his arm, she followed him toward the front gate. "The medics got here so quickly. I'm sure Mr. Bradley will be okay."

"I hope so," Robin murmured.

I should have strangled him while I had the chance, he told himself bitterly.

Meghan suddenly stopped. Her fingers dug into Robin's arm. "Who is that boy?" she whispered.

"Huh?" Robin turned to follow Meghan's gaze. "What boy?"

"That red-haired boy," she replied. "The tall, skinny one in the long, black T-shirt and baggy shorts."

Robin's eyes focused on the boy Meghan described. The red-haired boy quickly turned away.

"He was staring at us," Meghan reported.

"He was?" Robin studied the boy. He was tall and lanky. He looked a little like a stick figure, especially in the huge, baggy shorts. His red hair fell to his shoulders. He carried a bag of popcorn in one hand.

He glanced back at Robin. Seeing that Robin was staring at him, the boy instantly turned away again.

"He was staring at you as if he knew you," Meghan said.

"I've never seen him before," Robin replied. He pulled Meghan to the gate. "Let's get out of here."

"You don't know the truth about Robin Fear," the voice rasped into Dierdre's ear.

"Please—" Dierdre begged, gripping the phone so tightly her hand ached. "Leave me alone. Stop calling me. I—"

"I'm coming to see you," the voice threatened. *"I'm coming to tell you about Robin."*

"No! Please!" Dierdre begged.

The line went dead.

I've got to get to the hospital, she thought, her heart

pounding. The whispered voice still rasped in her ear, repeating its ugly threat.

"I'm coming to see you . . ."

I don't have time for this, Dierdre thought, slamming down the office phone. I've got to go see Daddy. Maybe today will be the day he wakes up.

The past few days had been so difficult for Dierdre. Staying hour after hour at the hospital. Talking to the doctors.

Sitting by her father's bed. Staring at the tubes and wires hooked up to his body. Waiting. Praying for him to open his eyes. To wake up.

Listening to his every breath. Wondering if he'd ever sit up. Ever smile. Wondering if she'd ever talk to him again.

So many hours at the hospital. So many tense, unhappy hours.

And afterward, Dierdre hurried to the park. She had so much to learn about running Fear Park. So much to learn and no time to learn it in.

The Ferris wheel was still closed down. But the rest of the park was operating normally. And crowds came every night.

Some people came to relax and have fun. Others came to view the scenes of horror.

I should start a Fear Park horror tour, Dierdre thought bitterly. The tour could start at the lion's area of the animal preserve. I could point out the spot where the preserve manager was torn apart and eaten by the lions.

Then we could move to where a bomb exploded in

the House of Mirrors. The flying shards of cut glass killed twelve people. That's a good stop on the tour.

And then we could end up at the Ferris wheel. I could show my customers where Daddy . . . where Daddy . . .

A sob burst from Dierdre's throat.

Such sick thoughts. She shook her head hard, as if trying to shake them from her mind.

She climbed up from her father's desk. Shoved in the desk chair. Stepped out of the trailer—and bumped into Robin Fear.

"Dierdre—hi. I was coming to see you."

His dark hair fell over his forehead. His dark, serious eyes stared into hers. He wore an oversize black Polo shirt over baggy chinos.

"Robin, I can't talk. I'm on my way to the hospital."

Robin placed a hand on her shoulder. "I just wondered how your dad is doing."

"I—I don't know," Dierdre stammered. She felt tears well up in her eyes. But she forced them back. "He's still in a coma, Robin."

The words didn't sound real to Dierdre. Was she really saying those words about her dad? Her big, strong bear of a dad?

Still in a coma.

"Well, what do the doctors say?" Robin asked, his eyes burning into hers.

Dierdre shrugged. "They don't know anything. They say he could wake up at any time and be fine. Or maybe never wake up. They—they . . ." She swallowed hard. It was so difficult to talk about it.

Robin shook his head sadly, lowering his gaze to the ground. "I'm so sorry. I feel so guilty, Dierdre. I tried to catch him as he fell. But I wasn't fast enough. I—I really feel responsible."

He's so sweet, Dierdre thought. So serious and caring and sweet.

"Robin—you can't blame yourself," she told him. "You can't. You did everything you could."

"And now the park will have to close," he said, his voice cracking with sadness. "I feel so awful for you, Dierdre. You worked so hard . . ."

"I'm keeping the park open," Dierdre announced.

Robin's mouth dropped open. "Excuse me?"

"I'm keeping it open," she repeated. "Daddy would want me to keep it open," she sighed. "Besides, I have no choice."

His dark eyes studied her face. "No choice?"

"We're broke," Dierdre blurted out. "We don't have a dime, Robin. I have to keep the park open—to pay Daddy's hospital bills. We don't even have insurance."

He let out a gasp, as if he'd been stabbed.

Robin cares so much about me, Dierdre thought. He's such a good friend. He's so upset for me. He actually looks wounded.

"If only I could help," he murmured.

Dierdre glanced at her watch. "I've got to run. I've got to get to the hospital."

She turned toward the front gate, then stopped. "I got another weird phone call," she told him.

Robin's eyes widened in surprise. "A phone call

about me? That's so sick. What did they say *this* time?"

"The same thing," Dierdre sighed. "Whoever it is said he was coming to tell me the truth about you."

She saw Robin's chin quiver. He bit his bottom lip.

"So sick," he murmured again. "So sick."

"You're right," she agreed. "Who could it be?"

Robin shrugged. "I have no idea. Why would someone want to warn you about me?"

"I'm a little scared," Dierdre admitted. "There are so many sick, twisted people in the world. What if—"

"It's just a stupid joke," Robin interrupted. "It *has* to be."

She saw the thoughtful expression on his face. Saw him clench his jaw.

"I've got to run," she told him. "Call me later?" She hurried away.

"Right. Later," he called after her.

Dierdre was trotting to the front gate when she saw the tall, lanky red-haired boy.

She stopped with a startled gasp.

He stared at her, a strange, lopsided grin on his face.

Her heart pounding, Dierdre stood still and waited for him to approach.

chapter
_____

9

Who is making those phone calls to Dierdre? Robin wondered, his mind whirring.

Who knows the *truth* about me?

It has to be the same person who sent her that newspaper clipping from 1935. The one with my picture.

Robin felt lucky he had been able to convince Dierdre it was a picture of his grandfather. But what if he weren't so lucky next time? He had to find out who was trying to warn her.

It isn't Meghan, he knew.

Meghan is completely fooled. Meghan would never do anything to ruin my plans. Because she doesn't know my real plans.

No. Not Meghan.

But then who?

Who else knows that I'm not really a teenager? Who

46

else would have that old newspaper story to send to Dierdre? Who else would be calling her?

A chilling thought almost made him cry out.

Had someone followed him from the past?

Had someone else from 1935 found a way to move to the future? Someone who knew the whole story? Someone eager to spoil Robin's plans?

Robin didn't want to think it possible. But it was the only answer.

What a shocking, horrible afternoon, Robin thought. First Dierdre breaks the awful news that she has decided to keep Fear Park open. Then he realizes that someone from the past is out to get him.

His mind spinning, Robin turned to leave.

He had gone only six or seven steps when he saw a red-haired boy giving Dierdre an awkward hug.

Was it the same boy Meghan had pointed out? Yes.

Robin stepped back into the shadow of the Bradleys' office trailer. He shielded his eyes from the bright sunlight that flooded over the gate.

Whoa! Robin thought. What is going on here?

How does Dierdre know that guy?

He crept deeper into the shadows. He didn't want either of them to see him.

Dierdre and the boy were both talking at once. Nervously, Robin thought. He squinted from the shadows into the sunlight. Yes. They both appeared very tense.

The red-haired boy kept shoving his hands into the pockets of his baggy shorts, then pulling them out again, then shoving them back in.

Dierdre shifted her weight uncomfortably from foot to foot.

Why are they so nervous? Robin wondered.

And then he decided: That boy is telling Dierdre something she doesn't want to hear. That's why she keeps glancing around and fidgeting.

That boy is telling her about me.

Despite the warmth of the day, Robin felt a chill. He knew he was staring at someone else from the past. Someone who had come to expose him and ruin his plans.

The boy swept back his long red hair and continued talking. Dierdre was shaking her head, her features drawn tightly, a frown on her face.

Who is he? How did he get here? Robin wondered. Did he come alone?

Robin narrowed his gaze on the boy's face. I don't remember him, he realized. I don't recognize him.

Meghan had seen the boy too. She hadn't recognized him either.

What were the two of them talking about so seriously?

Robin stood too far away to try to read their lips. If only there were some way to sneak up closer.

But they were in the middle of the open square that led to the front gate. If Robin stepped away from the trailer, they were certain to see him.

So Robin sank back in the shadows and watched. He didn't move until Dierdre and the boy started walking side by side to the gate.

They're leaving together! Robin saw. Together!

I've got to act fast, he decided. I can't let this boy—whoever he is—ruin all of my hard work.

Robin felt a sting. He reached up to the side of his face to swat a fly.

And a chunk of his cheek dropped off in his hand.

"Ohh." He let out a moan as he stared at the soft glob of flesh.

It's the tension, he realized. It's the worry. The fear.

I've got to solve this mystery right away. I've *got* to!

chapter
10

Robin hurried home to repair his face. Then he tried to read for a while. But he couldn't shake the red-haired boy from his mind.

Why don't I remember him? Robin wondered. Was he one of the kids who died on the work crew in 1935? If so, how did he figure out that my spell forced those kids to hatchet one another to death? How did he figure out that I was responsible?

If he died back then, how did he follow me to the future?

No, Robin decided. He couldn't have been on that work crew.

But, then, who is he?

Someone I knew back at Shadyside High?

A Bradley?

No, no, no. Robin pounded his fist against the wall.

The Bradleys don't know the dark arts. They don't know how to cast spells.

Did this boy make himself immortal? Robin wondered. Has he been following me all these years? Waiting for this moment to ruin all my plans?

Robin picked up the telephone. Maybe if he asked carefully, he could get some information from Dierdre. Maybe he could find out how much Dierdre knew.

He dialed her number at the trailer in the park. She picked it up after two rings.

"Hi, it's me," he told her. "I just wondered how you were doing."

"Well . . . I'm kind of busy right now, Robin."

He heard a new coldness in her voice. He recognized it instantly. Something has changed, he knew. *That red-haired boy told her about me. I can tell.*

"I thought maybe you and I could get together. Maybe tonight. You know. Near closing time."

Drumming his fingers on the table, he listened to the long silence at her end.

"I don't think so," she replied finally. Her tone was still distant. Icy. "It's so hard for me now," she continued. "I'm trying to keep the park going. And visit Daddy. And—"

"How is he?" Robin interrupted.

Is he dead yet? Please say yes.

"Still in a coma," Dierdre replied with a sigh. "Nothing has changed. The doctors . . . " Her voice trailed off.

"Well, the Ferris wheel is still closed. So I'm not working. I'll come by later," Robin told her. "Maybe you and I can—"

"I really don't think I can," she interrupted. Again

51

he heard the new coldness in her voice. "I'm sorry," she added.

She didn't sound sorry.

Is that fear I hear in her voice? Robin wondered.

Does she know the truth about me? And is she afraid of me now?

"Take it easy," he said, trying to sound sympathetic. "I know everything will be okay."

"Thanks, Robin. See you." Her reply was curt and cold.

He hung up.

He pictured the red-haired boy. And felt anger tighten his stomach. He swallowed hard, a sour taste in his mouth.

I've got to know if that boy is immortal. I've got to know if he is turning Dierdre against me.

It began to rain late that afternoon. A gentle summer rain that made the lawn sparkle like emeralds.

Robin glanced out the front window once, then pulled the heavy drapes shut. He felt like surrounding himself in darkness.

Bathing in darkness. So soothing.

Meghan was upstairs in her room. The only sound in the old house was the soft patter of rain against the window.

Should I tell Meghan that we've been followed? he asked himself.

He decided to wait. To wait until he was certain.

To wait until the boy had been taken care of.

The rain stopped just before dinnertime. He and

Meghan ate a quiet dinner. They hadn't much to talk about these days. They ate many meals in silence.

Both of us used to talk at once, he remembered with some sadness. We bubbled over. We laughed. We joked. We were so excited to be together. So happy.

Meghan looked as beautiful as ever, of course. The weekly treatments he gave her made sure that she never changed.

But he had no feeling left for her. No feeling at all.

She doesn't want to stay immortal. She wants to grow old and die, he knew.

Maybe he'd find a way to give her that wish. . . .

The sky had cleared. But the sidewalks still glistened from the day's rain as Robin made his way along Fear Street to the park. He felt a cold shock on the back of his neck as rainwater dripped from the trees.

As he neared the wide parking lot, he could hear music and voices from the park. He heard a shrill elephant trumpet from the wild animal preserve.

A line of people stood in twos and threes in front of the ticket booths. Many of them wore rain gear in case the storm picked up again.

Robin showed his pass and slipped into the park. The fountain in the main entryway sent up its colorful sprays. A hand-painted sign proclaimed that the park would remain open until eleven tonight.

Robin glared at the sign, surprised by his own anger.

Open till eleven? This park shouldn't be open at all,

he thought bitterly. I've worked so hard to close it down. And I have failed. Failed!

Until now, he added.

He snickered to himself. *No more Mr. Nice Guy,* he thought.

He came around the Bradleys' office trailer from the back. The long window up near the flat roof was dotted with rainwater. Robin stood on tiptoe to peer inside.

He saw Dierdre standing in front of the desk. She wore denim cutoffs and a pink midriff top. Her brown hair was pulled straight back and tied behind her head. She was talking rapidly, excitedly, gesturing with both hands.

Whom was she talking to?

Robin pressed up against the wet window glass to see.

He gasped.

The red-haired boy!

Robin dropped quickly and hunched down, hoping he hadn't been seen. His heart pounding, he made his way to the side of the trailer. And waited.

Who *is* this guy? What are they talking about so excitedly?

A few minutes later the trailer door swung open. Dierdre stepped out first. The red-haired boy followed.

Robin shrank into the shadows and watched them. They were walking close together, side by side, both of them talking at once.

Where were they headed?

Toward the rides area?

Careful not to get too close, Robin trailed after them. He strained to hear their words. But the music and other voices drowned them out.

They stopped to buy Cokes at a stand. Robin ducked around the side of the food booth. He heard Dierdre call the boy Gary.

Gary.

So now I know his name, Robin told himself. His brain was whirring. Gary. Gary. Did I know a Gary back in 1935?

No. I don't remember a Gary.

Pressing against the dark wall of the food stand, he watched them finish their Cokes. They still appeared nervous, tense.

What are they talking about? Robin wondered. Are they talking about me?

Gary tossed the two paper cups into a trash can. Then he tried to take Dierdre's hand. But she quickly pulled her hand away.

Robin caught disappointment on Gary's face.

Gary . . . Gary . . .

Robin struggled to remember. Was there a Bradley named Gary back in the 1930s? Did that creep Richard Bradley have a friend named Gary?

This is going to drive me crazy, Robin realized.

He followed Dierdre and Gary to the rides area. Bouncy calliope music floated over the park from the carousel at the end of the walkway. To Robin's left stood the Ferris wheel, dark and empty. Wooden sawhorses had been placed around it to keep people away.

His eyes on Dierdre and Gary, Robin nearly

tripped over a double baby stroller. The mother pushing the stroller yelled something at Robin. But he ignored her.

He dodged away and cut through a group of teenagers. He didn't want to lose sight of Dierdre and Gary.

His prey.

The hunter and his prey, Robin thought.

He watched them approach the Twirl 'n' Swirl. The ride was circular, like a merry-go-round. Around the circle were what looked like playground swings on very long metal lines. One person per swing.

When the ride started up, the swings began to move in a wide circle. Round and round, slowly at first. Then faster and faster—until the swings tilted out as they spun, flew out until they were almost horizontal with the ground.

Dierdre and Gary stood outside the low metal fence, watching the ride. As the swings picked up speed, the riders squealed and laughed. Some shot their hands up into the air. Others gripped the safety bars and held on tight.

Robin saw Dierdre laugh. She let Gary grab her arm and pull her into the short line of people waiting to get on next.

I don't understand this, Robin thought, studying their faces as he moved a little closer.

If he came to tell her the truth about me, why are they laughing and kidding around and going on rides?

The swings lowered as the ride spun slower. A few seconds later it slowed to a stop. Riders hopped off, smiling and laughing, and hurried dizzily to the exit gate.

Keeping in the shadows, Robin moved cautiously to the metal fence. He watched Dierdre and Gary climb into swings.

He watched them smile at each other. He watched Gary fiddle with the safety bar that dropped down over his waist.

That bar won't do you any good, Robin thought.

Unless you're immortal, Gary. Unless you *can't* be killed.

Robin shut his eyes and began to chant a spell.

Let's see *what* you are, Gary.

Let's see if you're immortal . . . or if you can be killed.

chapter
11

Someone was crying.

The shrill wails interrupted Robin's chant. He opened his eyes. Confused, he glanced quickly along the circle of swings.

Dierdre and Gary were sitting patiently, staring straight ahead, waiting for the ride to begin.

The cries grew louder.

Robin saw the attendant hurry over to a swing on the other side. He pulled up the safety bar and helped a little boy to the ground.

The boy had changed his mind at the last minute, Robin realized. He had decided the ride was too scary for him.

Robin chuckled to himself. That little guy doesn't know just *how* scary this ride is going to be!

The boy ran through the gate to his parents. The attendant ushered in a teenage girl to take the boy's place on the swing.

THE LAST SCREAM

All the swings were filled now, Robin saw. The attendant trotted over to the controls and threw the lever. The swings slowly began to move.

Robin shut his eyes and began to chant again.

Goodbye, Gary, he thought.

Goodbye—unless you are from the past. Unless you have somehow made yourself immortal.

Goodbye—unless you have come here to rescue Fear Park from my plans.

If you live through this, I will know that you are from the past.

And if that is the case, I will have to find another way to kill you. It won't be as easy, Robin told himself. But I will find a way.

I promise you, Gary. I will find a way. . . .

Dierdre gripped the safety bar and shifted her weight, trying to get more comfortable in the hard plastic seat. She watched the attendant push the lever and felt her swing move forward with a soft jolt.

She let go of the safety bar and folded her hands in her lap. She took a deep breath and prepared to enjoy the ride.

This is crazy, she thought.

I have too much work to do. Too much to worry about.

I don't have time in my life right now for fun. Why am I wasting my time on a silly swing ride?

Why did I let Gary talk me into this? Why am I here with him in the first place?

She glanced in his direction. But the swings were

swirling higher now, circling faster. She couldn't see him.

Gary is so strange, Dierdre thought.

It's as if he's from a different planet or something.

The strange things he talks about. Sometimes I don't know whether to believe him or not.

He frightens me. He really does.

So why am I sitting here, twirling around, riding the Twirl 'n' Swirl with him?

Dierdre's brown hair flew wildly around her head as the swing spun even faster. She reached up and tried to tug it into place—but quickly gave up when she saw that it was impossible.

Kids squealed and laughed as the swings spun faster.

Dierdre glimpsed Gary up ahead, his red hair flying, his hands straight up in the air. She called to him. But of course he couldn't hear her.

She gripped the safety bar and held on tightly as her swing spun out, tilted, horizontal to the ground now.

It really feels like flying, she thought. The rush of cold wind against her face made her smile. So refreshing.

But what is that strange purple smoke?

She glanced around, trying to see where the puffs of purple smoke were coming from. But she was whirling too fast to see anything clearly.

All a blur, she realized. A blur of dark sky and laughing faces—and purple . . . purple smoke.

Is that Gary up ahead?

60

She squinted through the purple as the car swung out even farther, spinning at full speed now.

And then she heard the loud *pop pop*.

She saw the lines snap. Saw the swing up ahead go flying.

Flying off by itself. Flying free.

Saw the lines pop off from the top. And the swing fly off.

Fly up.

"Noooooooo!" Dierdre's wail of horror was muffled by the onrush of air, by the clouds of thick purple smoke.

All a blur. All a purple blur.

But she could see the boy's hands flailing helplessly as the swing shot straight up.

Into the tight cluster of power lines.

Spinning, spinning, Dierdre craned her neck, struggled to see.

The boy's swing crashed into the power lines almost silently.

But then a sharp crackling sound rose up over the screams of the riders and crowd down below.

A sharp crackling sound. A buzz. And a flash of yellow light.

Dierdre saw the boy's hands and feet fly up against the power lines.

And then she saw his body outlined in bright yellow—crackling, bright yellow as the electricity sizzled around him.

His whole body twisted and jerked inside the buzzing yellow light.

And then the swing fell away, fell off the wires. Fell fast.

Dierdre knew when it landed. She could hear the sickening *crack*.

And then she shut her eyes and screamed and screamed and screamed.

chapter
12

Robin opened his eyes in time to see the lines on Gary's swing pop off. Squinting through the swirls of purple smoke, Robin watched Gary's swing float free.

A pleased grin spread over Robin's face as the swing shot up to the power lines. He saw the flash of electric current. Heard the sharp sizzle.

People screamed. Cries of horror rose up to drown out the electrical sizzle that shook Gary's body.

Robin watched Gary's arms and legs snap and twist helplessly. Watched as the bright current shot around Gary's body.

The swing appeared to stick up there forever. But it only stayed against the wires for a few seconds, Robin knew.

Long enough, he thought.

Long enough to fry Gary.

Then the swing fell quickly. Straight down.

People on the ground dove out of the way.

The swing landed with a hard *crack*. Inside the fence. On the far side. Away from Robin.

The purple smoke billowed and swirled. Then it started to fade.

Robin's heart pounded. Such excitement!

Kids were crying. People were running around the low fence, shouting and pointing in alarm. In horror.

The swings finally began to slow.

Robin smiled again. The attendant must have been too stunned to move, too shocked to stop the ride.

Robin watched the swings spin slower, slower. He searched for Dierdre. Was she the one screaming and waving her arms above her head?

Or was she the one tugging at her brown hair, head lowered, shoulders heaving?

"Dierdre, where are you?" Robin murmured out loud.

Dierdre, he thought happily, there seems to have been another tragedy at your amusement park.

Another horrifying accident.

Won't you give up now, dear Dierdre? Won't you close up the park? Pack up your things? Go to your poor father's bedside and care for him?

How many tragic accidents will it take, Dierdre?

The swings had finally slowed to a full stop. The dazed riders were lowering themselves to the ground, shaking their heads, crying, in shock.

Robin searched for Dierdre but didn't see her. More people went running across the field, hurrying to the fallen swing.

Shouts and cries tore through the air. In the distance, Robin heard the shrill wail of a siren.

Robin climbed over the low fence and joined the others running across the field. A crowd had already circled the fallen swing.

Murmurs of horror mixed with shrill cries of disbelief. Away from the crowd, a man leaned over the fence, vomiting loudly.

"Excuse me. Excuse me. Let me through." Robin had to fight his way through the crowd.

Pushing and bumping people out of his way, Robin forced himself to the front of the circle. Then he stared down at the broken swing.

Stared down at the broken, twisted body of the boy.

And gasped in shock. "No! No! I don't believe it!"

13

Robin swallowed hard. The ground seemed to tilt and sway, and he felt as if he might lose his balance.

He stared down at the pale face of the dead boy. The head tilted at such an odd angle. The boy's rib cage crushed beneath the safety bar of the swing.

Robin stared down at the boy, trying to make the face change. Trying to twist the features into the right shapes. Trying to change the nose, the blankly staring gray eyes. Trying to change the short blond hair to red.

But he couldn't make the face transform. He couldn't change the boy into Gary.

Feeling his heart flutter in his chest, Robin realized that he was staring down at a boy he had never seen before.

The wrong boy. He had killed the wrong boy.

Not Gary. Not Gary. Not Gary.

66

The words repeated like an ugly chant in Robin's mind.

Not Gary. Not Gary. Not Gary.

But *why* not Gary?

Confused, feeling shaky and weak—suddenly feeling his true age—Robin turned away from the crushed body.

His eyes searched the circle of onlookers. Their faces flashed red, then dark, red, then dark, as an ambulance pulled up, its light flashing.

"Move back! Move back!" somebody shouted.

Grim-faced police officers appeared. They raised black nightsticks in both hands and motioned with them, shouting orders, moving the crowd away from the fallen boy.

"Back! Everyone back! Now!"

"Make room! Make room for help to get through!"

Too late, Robin thought. Too late for help.

He saw a police officer staring at him, and he obediently began to back away. He stopped when he saw Dierdre.

She stood near the fence, away from the onlookers, huddled close to Gary. Gary had an arm around her shoulders. Robin couldn't see her expression. Her face was pressed against the front of Gary's shirt.

Gary. Not Gary. Gary. Not Gary.

Robin's mind whirred. The magic had never failed him before.

He blinked several times. But he couldn't make Gary disappear. He couldn't send Gary into the broken, fallen swing, where he belonged.

Gary leaned over Dierdre, tilting his face down to hers, his arm wrapped protectively around her.

What went wrong? Robin wondered.

Did I make a mistake? Did I simply make the wrong swing pop loose from its lines?

The swings were spinning so fast. It would be easy to make a mistake. To choose the wrong swing to send flying.

Is that what I did?

Or did Gary change swings at the last minute?

When I shut my eyes to begin the ancient chant, did he climb out of his swing and move quickly to another?

Or did I call up the spell incorrectly? Is it as simple as that?

A small mistake? Just a mistake?

Or did Gary survive because he has magic of his own?

Did Gary survive because he's immortal? Because he's from the past? Because he's *already dead*?

Cautiously, Robin made his way closer to Dierdre and Gary.

Police officers swarmed over the field, examining the swings. Near the fence, the boy's broken body had been covered with a canvas tarp. White-uniformed medics were lifting it on a stretcher into an ambulance.

Onlookers gathered in small groups. Some murmured softly. Others stared in shocked silence.

A TV reporter stepped into a bright spotlight. He straightened his tie and raised a microphone in one hand. "Are we rolling?" he kept repeating. "Are we rolling? Tell me when we're rolling."

White circles of light from police flashlights crisscrossed over the grass. Two more ambulances had pulled up to the ride, flashing red lights on their roofs casting an eerie, flickering glow over everyone.

Robin narrowed his eyes, trying to see clearly through the darting, flashing lights. He squinted hard across the grass at Dierdre.

And realized she was staring back at him.

With the coldest look on her face.

The icy stare made Robin turn away. Has Gary told her the truth about me? he wondered. Does she know *everything*?

chapter
14

"**D**o you remember the day the plants attacked you, Daddy?" Dierdre asked. The memory made her smile.

"Remember? Mom and I were in the den. You came in carrying a bowl of cereal. It must have been a weekend, since we were all home.

"I remember it was a beautiful morning," Dierdre continued. "I can picture the bright sunlight streaming in through the den windows. Remember? You said it would be even sunnier if Mom's plants didn't block the windows?

"And then you sat down in that big brown armchair you used to love. The one Mom said belonged in the cab of a truck. She always wanted to put that chair in the attic, but you would never let her.

"Anyway, you sat down in the chair, remember? You leaned back and raised the cereal bowl in one hand. And that's when the plants attacked.

"They were vines. Two pots of big vines. I remember how big and shiny the leaves were. You remember how Mom took care of those plants. She'd spend half a day just on the plants in the den.

"Anyway, those vines seemed to reach around the sides of the chair. Both vines moved at the same time. It looked as if they were reaching for you.

"You were so shocked. You jumped up and spilled the cereal all over the floor. All over *you* and the floor. 'They attacked me!' you screamed. 'Those plants of yours—they attacked me!'

"Mom and I started laughing, and we couldn't stop," Dierdre recalled, wiping a tear from one eye. "I guess it was because you looked so serious. You really thought the two vines were attacking you!

"Of course, the window was open. And the wind blew the vines onto your chair. But you were convinced the plants were attacking you. 'It's a jungle in here! A jungle!' you shouted.

"And Mom pretended to get really offended. Because you know how much she loved her plants. She loved tending them, watering them, cutting them back. She loved caring for them. I guess it made her feel peaceful. I guess plant time was her peaceful time of day—don't you think?

"Well, after that Mom and I had to laugh every time you came into the den and sat down in that chair. We could just picture the vines attacking you again. It made us laugh every time.

"Of course, after Mom died . . ." Dierdre's voice caught in her throat. "Well, I understood that you didn't have time to care for all the plants. I understood why the plants had to go.

"I guess they probably reminded you too much of Mom, huh, Daddy? But it made me sad. It made **me** so sad to walk into the den and not see it crammed with green plants. It was as if so much life had been taken from the house.

"Do you know what I mean, Dad? Mom's life—and then the plant life . . . So much life had been taken away from us. Do you hear me, Daddy? Can you hear me at all?

"Or am I talking to myself? Am I just making myself cry? Remembering what our lives used to be like when Mom was alive. And when you . . . when you . . . "

A sob escaped Dierdre's throat. She wiped away another tear tracking down her cheek.

She leaned over the smooth white sheets of the hospital bed and squeezed her father's hand. It felt so soft, so cold, so lifeless in her hand.

"Can you hear me at all, Daddy?" she whispered.

The tubes attached to Mr. Bradley gurgled as if in reply. But Dierdre's father didn't move, didn't blink, didn't move or make a sound.

Dierdre stared down at her father. He had been in the hospital for less than two weeks. But already his cheeks were sunken and pale. He had always been so robust, so alive. And now his face looked almost skeletal.

His eyes remained shut, the eyelids fluttering from time to time but not opening. His chest rose with each breath, a soft wheeze escaping his white lips.

Dierdre had spent the morning with the family lawyer at the Shadyside police station. They answered question after question about safety precautions and maintenance of the Twirl 'n' Swirl.

"How did this accident occur?" the lieutenant kept demanding. "How did *two* lines on the swing pop loose at once?"

Dierdre had no answer for him.

She arrived at the hospital shortly after lunch. She had eagerly found Dr. Bruhn in his office. "Any change? Did Daddy wake up?"

The young doctor scratched his smooth, beardless jaw. "Not yet," he told her. "But his vital signs remain good."

What did that mean? she wondered.

"Can't you tell me when Daddy might wake up? Can't you give me any idea at all?" Dierdre demanded shrilly.

Dr. Bruhn shook his head. He gave a slight shrug of his narrow shoulders. "I wish I knew, Dierdre. There's just no answer to that question."

"When he wakes up . . ." Dierdre started to say. "Will he be okay? I mean, after being in a coma for so long, will his mind be . . . the same?"

A sigh escaped the young doctor's lips. "I can't answer that one either," he replied with some sadness.

He climbed to his feet and stepped around the cluttered desk. He placed a hand gently on Dierdre's shoulder. "We can only hope for the best. We have to—"

"But when will he wake up?" Dierdre demanded. "When?"

"The brain has a natural healing ability," the doctor replied softly, his hand still resting on Dierdre's shoulder. "Sometimes it takes days for a coma patient to come out of it. Sometimes weeks. Sometimes . . ." His voice trailed off.

Dierdre opened her mouth to talk, but no sound came out. She cleared her throat. "Dr. Bruhn—"

"Go see your father," the doctor instructed. "Go talk to him. He can probably hear you, Dierdre. Your voice will mean a lot to him. Even if he doesn't hear the words, your voice will mean a lot."

The doctor returned to his desk chair. Dierdre stood up shakily.

"We are monitoring him carefully. We have every hope," he told her. And then he added, "Be brave."

"Be brave."

The words followed her down the twisting, pale green halls of Shadyside General.

"Be brave."

She took a deep breath and stepped into her father's room. Pulled a folding chair up to his bedside. The sheets so smooth and unwrinkled.

Smooth and unwrinkled because he *didn't move.*

She took his hand, his soft, lifeless hand. And she started to talk to him. Holding back the tears that tried to force their way from her eyes, holding back the sobs, holding back the *screams,* she began to talk.

And remember.

She remembered the story about the den plants, and she told it to him, leaning close, so close she could smell the piney smell on his skin from the soap the nurses used to wash him.

She told him other stories, talking softly, just above a whisper. Squeezing his hand—his baby hand—as she talked.

As she talked, Dierdre noticed a shadow moving across the window. She could hear a low roar from outside. It seemed to rise and fall in rhythm with the shadow.

She moved to the window to investigate. Her father's room was on the first floor. Across the parking lot, Dierdre could see two tall bulldozers. Their enormous shovels rose up in unison, like two elephants raising their trunks at a waterhole. Dierdre could see them filled with large chunks of rock. Probably making the parking lot bigger, she realized.

"Well, the noise doesn't bother you—does it, Daddy?" she asked sadly. She dropped back into the chair beside his bed.

The tubes gurgled. A heart monitor pulsed steadily against the wall.

Dierdre slumped against the hard chair back. "I'm glad you can't hear some things," she told her father, struggling to keep her voice low and steady. "I'm glad you can't hear about the accident at the park last night."

Did his eyelids flutter? No. Dierdre studied her father's face. He didn't move.

"I'm glad you can't hear about one more innocent person dying at Fear Park," Dierdre continued, unable to hide her emotion. "I don't understand it, Daddy. I really don't. People say the land is cursed. Maybe it's true. Maybe it really is. But I think—"

Dierdre stopped when she heard a scraping sound behind her from the door.

She spun around quickly as a figure stepped into the room.

"Huh? What are *you* doing here?" she cried.

chapter
15

Robin tried to hide his surprise. But a loud gasp escaped his throat.

He struggled to keep his expression calm and unrevealing. "Dierdre!" he cried. "I didn't expect—"

No. He didn't expect her to be here.

He expected Dierdre to be at the police station, answering questions about the tragic accident of the night before.

Having Dierdre in her father's room did not fit in at all with Robin's plan. A simple plan. A plan to finish what he had started back at the Ferris wheel.

Robin had come to the hospital to murder Mr. Bradley.

He is so weak, it will not take long, Robin had reasoned. I'll either squeeze my fingers over the air tube. Or else smother him with a pillow.

When her father is dead, Dierdre will be left with

no hope at all. Then she will have to give up and close Fear Park.

But now, there she stood.

Ruining Robin's plan. Blocking his way once again. Glaring at him coldly.

"Robin? What are you doing here?" she repeated.

"I . . . uh . . . came to see how your dad was doing," he told her. He stepped up beside Dierdre and gazed down at Mr. Bradley. "I've been thinking about him a lot," Robin continued softly. "Thinking about that horrible day at the Ferris wheel. How I could have saved him. But . . ." Robin forced his voice to crack.

"You shouldn't blame yourself," Dierdre replied, keeping her eyes on her father. "You can't blame yourself for an accident, Robin."

Why did she stare straight ahead so icily? Robin wondered. Why didn't she talk to him with the same feeling, the same warmth, as before?

He knew the answer.

Gary.

Outside the window, he heard the roar and grind of construction equipment. A squeal. Then a crash as rocks tumbled from their large front claws.

"He . . . hasn't woken up?" Robin asked softly, ignoring Dierdre's coldness.

Dierdre shook her head. She bit her lower lip.

"What do the doctors say?" Robin asked.

"They don't know anything," Dierdre replied bitterly.

"Don't they have any idea—" Robin started to ask.

Dierdre turned to him, her chin quivering. "I . . . I really don't feel like talking."

Robin took a step back. "Okay. I'm sorry. I—"

"It was really nice of you to come." She said the words automatically, with no feeling at all. When she raised her eyes to him, they held no warmth.

"Well, if there's anything I can do . . ." Robin said.

There's a lot I *could* do, he thought. If only you weren't here, Dierdre.

"Thank you," she replied stiffly. Then she narrowed her eyes at him. "Were you in the park last night?"

The question caught Robin by surprise.

Didn't she see me there by the Twirl 'n' Swirl? Didn't she glare at me so coldly while she held on to Gary?

It was so dark. And all those lights were flashing, he realized.

Maybe she didn't see me.

"No," he told her. "I wasn't there. But I saw what happened. On the news. I feel so bad for you, Dierdre. Really. I—"

She turned back to her father.

Before Gary, she would have rushed into my arms, Robin thought bitterly.

Before Gary, she would have turned to me for comfort. She would have confided in me.

Before Gary, she trusted me.

And now . . .

"I'll talk to you later," he said. "I hope everything works out."

For *me*. Not for you! he thought angrily.

He turned and hurried out of the room. His shoes thudded noisily on the hard floor as he made his way quickly through the twisting green halls.

Bright sunlight forced him to shield his eyes as he pulled open the side door and stepped out onto the parking lot. He squinted into the glare, waiting for his eyes to adjust.

And saw Gary leaning against a blue Honda Civic near the back of the lot.

He's following me, Robin realized.

Watching me.

Waiting for me.

Does he really think I'll let him do this? Robin wondered, squinting into the hot white glare of sunlight. The heat sent shimmering waves up from the parking lot.

Gary, in a pale blue muscle shirt and denim cutoffs, leaned casually against the car hood. His long red hair caught the light of the sun. His whole head glowed as if on fire.

Does he really think I'll stand here and let him spy on me? Robin asked himself. Does he think he can follow me wherever I go?

What does he think he's doing?

Hasn't he already done enough damage? Hasn't he told Dierdre the truth about me? Turned her against me?

He has done what he came to do. Why is he still hanging around?

Gary shoved himself up from the car. He stretched.

Is he coming over here? Robin wondered. He stepped back into the shelter of the hospital doorway.

Gary brushed back his long, coppery hair with both hands. He kicked a front tire on the blue car.

He's trying to fool me, Robin realized. He wants to make me think that he's not interested in me. He's pretending that he isn't watching me.

What an idiot.

The sunlight beamed down on Robin, but he felt only cold.

Cold hatred.

I won't let this idiot spoil my plans.

The steam shovels roared behind Gary. They dug into the rocky patch beside the parking lot. And rose up, carrying a full load of heavy gray rock.

As they dumped the load of rocks and turned to grab up more, Robin had an idea.

He stepped out into the parking lot. Shielding his eyes from the sunlight, he began to chant.

Do I remember this spell? he asked himself.

I think I do. I think I can get it right.

Right enough to take care of Gary.

Were you just lucky last night, Gary? Robin wondered.

You're not immortal, are you? You don't have any special magic. You were just lucky last night—right?

"Let's find out," Robin murmured out loud. "Let's find out the truth once and for all."

He shut his eyes and began to chant. He chanted slowly, softly, struggling to remember the words.

When he opened his eyes, purple smoke swirled

thickly over the parking lot. Snakes of purple slithered between the shimmering rays of golden sunlight.

Robin continued to chant, watching the purple smoke rise over the cars. The parking lot appeared to darken as the swirling smoke thickened to block the light.

Chanting softly, Robin glimpsed Gary through the heavy, dark mist. And he saw the steam shovels roll up behind Gary. Saw them raise their heavy loads.

Yes! It's working! Robin saw.

And then a heavy curtain of purple smoke cut off his view.

Robin couldn't see his victim. Couldn't see the approaching machines.

But over the whisper of his chants, Robin heard the grind and roar of the big machines.

Then he heard the loud rumble of the heavy stones as they toppled down, down from the twin claws of the powerful steam shovels.

Robin grinned as he heard Gary's startled scream.

chapter

17

The purple smoke swirled around him, so thick and heavy Robin felt as if he were underwater. He tried to run across the lot. He was eager to see Gary buried under a mountain of rock.

But the smoke spread and billowed, as if pushing him back.

Robin heard another loud scream. Then running footsteps.

Pinpricks of yellow sunlight penetrated the swirling purple fog. Then sharp beams of bright light cut through the thick darkness.

As the smoke began to fade, pushed away by the streaming, bright sunlight, Robin rubbed his eyes. He started toward the pile of rocks at the back of the lot.

Halfway across the lot, he stopped when he heard voices behind him.

"Huh?" Robin spun around.

In time to see Gary rush up to Dierdre as she stepped out of the hospital door.

"Whoa!" Robin cried out in shock.

Gary? How could Gary—?

What is going on here?

I heard Gary's cry as the rocks fell on him, Robin thought. I heard him scream. I heard it so clearly.

Another scream made Robin jump.

Turning back to the steam shovels, Robin saw the two operators jump down from their machines. They were screaming at each other, gesturing wildly with their hands.

It wasn't Gary who screamed when the rocks came tumbling down, Robin realized. I heard one of the operators scream.

And now the two men were screaming angrily at each other, pointing to the pile of rocks that had been dropped where they weren't supposed to be.

And Gary was running up to greet Dierdre.

Gary, safe and sound, was greeting Dierdre.

"I've been waiting for you," Robin heard him say. "I thought you might need a ride."

Waiting for Dierdre?

No. No way. Robin knew better.

Robin knew that Gary had been waiting for *him*. Keeping a close watch on *him*.

Why?

Robin wasn't sure.

He ducked behind a car. He didn't want Dierdre and Gary to see him studying them.

His mind spun. He felt dazed. The bright sun seemed to make him dizzy.

What had just happened here? Robin realized that he wasn't sure of anything.

Had Gary used magic to escape the tumbling rocks? Or was he just lucky? Did Gary start to run to the hospital door just as the rocks began to fall?

Magic or luck?

Was Gary an immortal from the past or just a very lucky human?

Robin had tried to kill him twice—and failed twice. *Could* Gary be killed?

Robin hated feeling so confused, so unsure.

I've run out of patience, he realized. It's time to finish this drama.

You're not going to win, Gary. If you have come from the past to ruin my plans, you are not going to win.

I'll see to that.

I guess I've put off killing Dierdre because a part of me actually likes her.

But if I am going to shut down Fear Park, I can't put that unpleasant task off any longer.

Leaning against the car, Robin pulled himself up and peered around, making sure Dierdre and Gary had left. He started to stand up—when two hands grabbed him roughly by the shoulders and spun him around.

chapter

18

Robin stared into the angry red face of a middle-aged man who looked more like a bulldog than a human.

"Hey—let go of me!" Robin cried.

The man kept his tight grasp on Robin's shoulders. He narrowed his tiny round eyes accusingly at Robin. "What were you doing to my car?" he growled.

"Huh? Your car?" Robin glanced back at the car he'd been hiding behind.

The bulldog face reddened to a deep scarlet. "Stealing my car?"

"No! No way!" Robin protested. "I—I dropped a quarter on the ground. I just bent down to pick it up. Really, sir!"

I'm over eighty years old, Robin thought angrily. And I have to stand here acting like a frightened teenager, calling this big idiot "sir"!

"I—I didn't touch your car!" Robin added.

The tiny eyes glared at Robin for a few seconds more. Then the man's big fists slowly loosened their hold.

The man grunted, as if to show that he was satisfied with Robin's story. The deep scarlet faded on his face. He turned to his car, studying it with his eyes, then rubbing a hand over the passenger door.

Robin's heartbeat returned to normal. He started to think clearly again.

He remembered a spell that brought a smile to his face. *I'll glue this big jerk to his car. I'll glue his skin to the car so that he cannot be removed. He and his car can stick together for the rest of his life.*

Glancing up, Robin saw two white-uniformed nurses watching him from the next aisle. A hospital guard was hurrying across the lot toward him.

Forget the spell, Robin thought. *I've got more important problems to deal with.*

The big man grunted again. "Sorry, kid. I saw you leaning on the car and—"

"No problem," Robin interrupted. He turned quickly and trotted away.

He waited at the bus stop, shielding his eyes from the bright sun, thinking about Dierdre.

Dierdre and Gary.

What a disappointing afternoon, he thought.

Maybe tonight will be more successful . . .

"Robin, you promised," Meghan sighed. She tossed her jacket on a living room chair and dropped down on the chair arm.

"Not yet," Robin replied impatiently. "I'm not ready yet."

He closed the book he'd been reading and gazed across the room at her. She had both hands raised to the back of her red hair. She was fixing a braid that had come loose.

Late afternoon shadows slid across the carpet from the front window. Meghan appeared half in shadow, half in light. Her emerald eyes glowed dully.

"Where were you?" he asked.

She sighed again. "Just out for a walk." She tugged at her hair, tilting her head against the shoulder of her olive sweater. "I'm so bored."

"I know," he murmured. "Maybe you need a hobby." He chuckled. He didn't mean it seriously. He just wanted to avoid their usual conversation about how bored she was, how she wanted to grow old.

I'm so bored with *you,* Meghan, he thought, studying her.

"You promised you'd find a spell," she started to complain. "You promised you'd find a way to let me grow old."

"Yes, yes." He couldn't keep the irritation from his voice. How many times do we have to have this conversation? he wondered.

"If *you* want to stay a teenager forever—fine," she told him. "But I can't take it anymore, Robin. Let me grow old without you."

"We'll go together. I don't want to live without you," he said.

What a lie, he thought bitterly.

"Let's do it now," she urged, lowering her hands

from the braid. As she leaned toward him, her face moved from light to shadow. "I can't stand living in two worlds anymore. I'm old and I'm young at the same time. But I don't belong in either world. I have no friends. No real life. No purpose. I have only you . . ."

"That used to be enough," Robin murmured, surprised at his own bitterness.

"But I'm not real," Meghan protested. "Can't you understand? I'm a ghost. A living ghost. I'm not at home anywhere. Not even inside my own body!" A sob escaped her throat.

She leaned into the light, then back into shadow, her eyes on Robin. She nibbled her bottom lip, waiting for his reply.

He gazed back at her. She shifted uncomfortably. Now half in shadow, half in light.

"I'll find a spell," Robin replied wearily. "I promise."

"When?"

"When my work is finished here," he said firmly.

"But you can't save the park," Meghan protested. "You can't save it, Robin. You've tried and tried. But your father's curse is stronger than you, stronger than your powers."

Robin forced himself not to laugh in her face.

With everything that has happened, he thought, Meghan remains loyal. Stupid and loyal.

She still believes I'm here to help the Bradleys. She really believes I'm trying hard to save Fear Park.

I'm going to miss her, he thought. She's pitiful. But I'm going to miss her.

Meghan startled him by jumping to her feet. "Why are you grinning?" she demanded sharply.

"Huh? Me?" He hadn't realized that a smile had crept over his face.

"You're grinning!" she accused him.

"No. Really. I'm not."

"You're laughing at me—aren't you!" she cried. "You think I'm funny?" Her green eyes suddenly glowed with anger.

"No, Meghan—stop," he said calmly, motioning with both hands for her to sit back down.

"You're still smirking!" she screeched.

"Meghan—"

She crossed the room, her fists balled at her sides. Robin jumped to his feet. He raised his hands as if to shield himself. He had seen her fiery temper before.

"You don't take me seriously at all—*do* you, Robin?" she cried, bumping up against him, nearly knocking him back into his chair.

"Meghan, please—"

"You've been laughing at me this whole time. You have no intention of doing what I ask. You're never going to let me escape from this horrible life—are you? Are you?"

She didn't wait for a reply. With a wild shriek she raised both fists—and began to pound his chest.

"Get off!" he cried. "Stop it! Stop it, Meghan! Listen to me. I—"

"Shut up! Shut up! Shut up!" She shoved him hard. Then she slapped his face.

"Oww!" He uttered a howl of pain and stumbled back.

He struggled to catch his balance—but she slapped him again.

He gasped as he saw a chunk of his skin fly off in her hand.

"Sssstop!" he hissed furiously. "I'm warning you—"

"No! No! No!" In her fury she grabbed at his other cheek and snatched off another chunk of skin.

"My face!" Robin shielded himself with one arm. "You're pulling off my face!"

"I don't care!" Meghan wailed. "I don't care! I don't care about *anything* anymore!"

She made a wild grab for him.

He ducked. Shoved her away.

His arm shot back. Without thinking, he slammed a fist into the side of her face.

"Oh!"

They both cried out in surprise. He had never hit her before.

The force of his punch tore off a wide section of her cheek. Gray bone poked out from the long skin tear.

"Aaaaiiiii!" With a shout of wild fury, she leapt on him. Clawed at his face. Clawed frantically with both hands.

Ripping off skin and flesh. Pulling off a chunk of his chin. Tearing at his nose.

Groaning in pain, in horror, Robin threw both fists up. One fist caught Meghan under the chin. The skin tore off cleanly, revealing gray jawbone and a line of bottom teeth.

"Noooooo!" Meghan uttered a long, pained howl— and sank her teeth deep into Robin's throat.

THE LAST SCREAM

Grabbing, ripping, tearing at each other, they fell to the floor, rolling over chunks of their own flesh as they wrestled and fought.

What on earth are we doing? Robin wondered.

Are we going to tear each other to pieces?

chapter
19

Dierdre's new friend had told Dierdre
all she needed to know about Robin Fear.

Of course, Dierdre hadn't believed it at first.

Who would believe such a wild story?

But now Dierdre was convinced. She believed it all.

Robin's father, Nicholas Fear, had placed a curse
on the park. And Robin had made himself immortal.
Had stayed a teenager. Had become Dierdre's friend.
Closer than a friend.

Robin had done all this to make sure that Nicholas
Fear's curse was carried out. To make sure that Fear
Park closed so that the land would be returned to the
Fear family.

Dierdre stared at herself in her dresser mirror.
"You don't look stupid," she told herself sternly. "But
you are."

She shook her head fretfully, watching her unhappy

reflection. "How could you let yourself be fooled by him?" she scolded herself. "How could you let yourself get so close to him? You actually thought you were in *love* with him!"

That thought made her cheeks redden.

"Stupid, stupid, stupid."

Robin must think you're the stupidest person on earth.

I confided in him, Dierdre moaned to herself. I trusted him. I *believed* in him.

I *kissed* him. I *cared* about him.

And all the time he was plotting against me. Plotting to destroy Daddy and me and ruin Fear Park.

He's a murderer. Robin is a cold, cold murderer.

So many lives lost. So many innocent lives . . .

He murdered children. He murdered young people.

He murdered people who had just come to the park to have a little fun.

Dierdre shuddered.

She had so many horrifying pictures in her mind, pictures that would stay with her for the rest of her life—all because of Robin Fear.

He doesn't care about human life, she realized, shivering again. And why should he?

He's fixed it so that he will live forever. Death has no meaning for him.

He doesn't care who lives . . . who dies.

I was so stupid. So trusting and stupid.

And if her new friend hadn't warned her . . .?

What would have happened?

Dierdre sank onto her bed.

What *will* happen? she wondered.

Is there any way to win this battle? *Can* Robin Fear be defeated?

Or am I going to die too?

chapter

20

"**H**old still. I'm almost finished."

Robin smoothed the skin over Meghan's cheek with two fingers. Then he brought his face close to hers and studied his handiwork.

"How does it look?" Meghan asked softly.

Robin gave her the oval hand mirror. She raised it, moved toward the bathroom light, and studied her face.

"Like new." She smiled.

"No—don't smile!" Robin warned. "You'll crease it. Give it time to dry."

Meghan forced her lips to cooperate. She watched her face grow completely expressionless. "It itches a little," she told him.

"It will probably itch until it's dry," he replied. He took the hand mirror and studied his own face. He tsk-tsked, shaking his head, watching himself in the mirror.

"I'm not happy with this chin," he murmured. "I think it may be too long."

Meghan turned and examined the chin. "It's fine. Listen . . ." Her voice trailed off.

She brushed past him into the hallway. "I—I'm sorry," she stammered.

"It's okay," he replied, still gazing at his new chin.

"I didn't mean to cause you so much work," she continued. "I mean, I shouldn't go berserk. It's just . . . well . . ."

"I understand," Robin said curtly. He didn't feel like starting another discussion.

"I had to get you to listen to me," Meghan said, rubbing both cheeks gently with the backs of her hands. "I had to let you see that I really mean it this time."

Robin nodded. "I promise," he said, staring into the mirror. "I promise I'll reverse your immortality spell—as soon as I can."

"Robin—as soon as you can? What does that mean?"

"I want to try one more time to help the Bradleys," he replied. "I want to try one more time to break the curse."

He lowered the mirror and turned to her. "You have to understand, Meghan. All those people have died in Fear Park. And I feel responsible. I mean, I *know* it wasn't my fault. I know it was my father's fault. But I feel guilty all the same."

He sighed. "And if there's anything I can do to break the curse—anything at all—I'm going to try it."

He stared deeply into her green eyes, intent on seeing if she still believed him.

Yes!

She still believes me, he realized.

He kissed her forehead. The new skin hadn't quite dried. It felt sticky and moist against his lips.

"I'm sorry too," he whispered. "We both lost control. It was my fault too."

She smiled. "I'm a pretty good wrestler," she said.

"Too good!" he replied. With one final glance at the repair job on his face, he stepped into the hallway and headed to his room.

"Where are you going?" she called after him.

"To the park," he told her. "This may be an important night. A very important night."

He pulled on a long-sleeved plaid shirt over his T-shirt. He wiped a small chunk of skin off one knee of his jeans. He had an idea.

Turning to the doorway, he saw Meghan watching him, arms crossed in front of her. "Do you remember a boy named Gary?" he asked casually.

She twisted her face, thinking. "Gary? From when?"

"From our class. You know. Back in 1935."

She tapped her chin. "Gary. Gary . . ." She sighed. "It's so hard to remember, Robin. My memory of those days is so faded. It was so long ago. I can't remember."

"Well, *try,*" he demanded sharply.

"Hmmmm." She tapped her chin some more, her eyes shut. "Yes," she said finally. "There *was* a Gary. Gary Barth."

"Gary Barth?" Robin struggled to remember him. But no face came to mind.

"Yeah. Gary Barth," Meghan said. "I remember him now. He was very tall, very thin and lanky."

"What color hair did he have?" Robin asked.

"Red hair," she replied. "Long, straight red hair. Down to his shoulders."

"That's him!" Robin cried. "That's him!"

chapter
21

"**Y**our father's condition remains unchanged," the nurse said in a low, flat tone. "We have your phone number. We'll call you if there is any change."

"Thank you," Dierdre replied. "Good night." She replaced the receiver with a sigh. Then she propped her elbows on her father's desk and dejectedly rested her head in her hands.

His condition remains unchanged.

Is that good or bad? she wondered unhappily.

I guess it means Daddy isn't getting any worse.

But why doesn't he wake up? The doctors say they cannot fully check him for brain damage until he wakes up.

Dierdre swallowed hard, her throat dry, achy. *What if he never wakes up?*

She sighed. Then, at least, he will never have to know that all of his problems were caused by the Fear family. He will never have to know that this park—his dream—was cursed from the start.

A knock on the office trailer door made Dierdre jump. She sat straight up, wheeled the desk chair around to face the door. "Who is it?"

The door swung open. Robin Fear poked his head in. "Busy?"

His smile made her want to throw up.

Without realizing it, she grabbed the silver letter opener from the desk and gripped it tightly in her fist. I'd like to plunge this through his heart, she thought.

I'd like to stab him through the heart and say, "This is for what you did to my father!" And then stab him again and again for all the people he killed here in the park.

He climbed into the trailer, still smiling. "You okay? I asked if you were busy," he said.

How could I ever fall for him? Dierdre asked herself. How could I ever *love* him? Just seeing him makes me sick now.

"Yeah. Very busy," she replied sharply. She turned to the desk and shuffled some papers around.

"How about a short walk?" he asked. "Get some fresh air. It's a really pretty night."

"Can't," she mumbled, shuffling papers, eyes on the desk.

Where is Gary? she wondered. He promised to meet me. He promised to stay with me, in case . . .

"Come on, Dee." Robin grabbed her arm gently. "A short walk. Five minutes. I promise it will change your mood."

His touch made her shudder. "My mood is okay," she replied coldly.

"Come on," he insisted. His grip on her arm tightened. He slid his hands down and grabbed both of her hands. And tugged. "Come on. A five-minute walk."

Let go of me! she thought.

Let go of me!

She glanced up. Caught the hard stare on his face. So cold. So cold and hard.

What is he doing? she wondered, suddenly gripped with fear.

What is he going to do to me?

"Let go of me—"

chapter
22

"**A** short walk," Robin repeated, dragging Dierdre to the trailer door.

"Ow!" She cried out as she bumped her side on the sharp corner of the desk.

He laughed. "Sorry."

Dierdre wanted to reach down and rub her aching side. But Robin wouldn't let go of her hand.

What should I do? she asked herself. Should I scream for help? That wouldn't do much good. I'd only look silly. How could I convince anyone I am in real danger?

Should I scream at Robin? Force him to let go of me? Tell him I'm never walking with him again?

No. I don't want him to know that I know the truth about him.

And I definitely don't want to make him any angrier.

Maybe I'd better take the walk with him, Dierdre

decided. After all, I'll be a lot safer in the middle of a crowd. I'll be a lot safer in public than alone in this trailer with him.

"Okay. I'm coming. I'm coming!" she cried, forcing herself to sound playful. "You just won't take no for an answer, *will* you!"

Robin laughed. "No way." He helped her down the trailer steps.

She followed him into a cool, clear night. Slender wisps of black clouds snaked across a low half moon. The air carried the aroma of fresh-popped popcorn.

Dierdre took a deep breath. She felt Robin's eyes on her, so she forced a smile. She glanced quickly around, searching for Gary.

Where is he? Where is he? He promised he'd be here.

Robin took her hand. He brought his face close to hers. "This way," he said softly.

She reluctantly allowed him to lead her. As they walked, holding hands, she studied his face, trying to read his thoughts.

What is he planning?

Staring hard at him, Dierdre thought something looked different about him. Was it his eyes? The smoothness of his skin? His expression? Something had changed.

Gary, where are you? she wondered, feeling her stomach knot up. How could you leave me alone with him?

"Where are we going?" She tried to keep her voice steady. But the words came out tense and strained.

"Just for a walk," he replied coyly. "Don't you like to walk with me anymore?"

She forced herself to squeeze his hand. "Of course I do," she cooed.

I can't let him know that I know everything about him.

I can't let him know. He'll kill me too. I know he will.

If he doesn't already plan to do that right now . . .

She shivered.

He turned to her, suspicion in his eyes. "Are you feeling okay? You keep shivering."

She shrugged. "Yeah. I'm fine. It's kind of chilly tonight."

His dark eyes remained locked on hers. His smile faded. "Is there anything you want to tell me? Anything you want to talk about?"

She shook her head. "No. Really. I'm just . . . you know . . . so worried about my dad."

Robin nodded solemnly. "Any word from the hospital? Any news?"

"No." Dierdre sighed. "He's the same. He hasn't woken up."

Dierdre was shocked by the smile that crossed Robin's face. *He isn't even trying to hide his true feelings!* she realized. *He isn't even pretending to be concerned.*

What does this mean?

She glanced nervously around. They were on the trail that led to the animal preserve. Since the preserve was closed at night, the path was dimly lit and nearly empty. No one else in sight.

THE LAST SCREAM

Why is he leading me here, where there are no people? Dierdre wondered. I don't want to go this way. I don't want to be all alone with him.

She took a deep breath. Turned quickly. And started to run.

chapter
23

"Hey—" Robin cried. "Dierdre?"

Where is she going? he wondered. Does she really think she can run away from me?

He hesitated for a second, watching her run. Then he took off after her, his sneakers thudding hard on the paved path.

She knows everything, he realized.

I can see it on her face. In her icy stares. I can hear it in her voice.

Gary told her everything. She knows the truth. The truth about me, about my father's curse, about why I am here.

She knows I will not rest until Fear Park is destroyed.

She knows she is helpless against me.

So why is she running? Why can't she accept her fate? Why won't she close the park—and save her own life?

He saw her turn onto the main walkway. Red, blue, and yellow lights glowed from the trees overhead. A wash of color made the park brighter than daylight.

Robin wanted to stay in the darkness near the animal preserve. He didn't want to go this way.

As he ran after Dierdre, the lights seemed to swirl around him, making the food stands and game booths spin and tilt.

He blinked and sucked in a deep breath, trying to regain his balance. "Dierdre?" he called to her breathlessly.

She kept running, pushing her way through a group of young men on their way to the shooting gallery. She didn't turn back.

"Dierdre?"

The bright lights burned his eyes.

Out of control, he thought. I feel so out of control tonight.

It's all slipping away, he thought unhappily. His chest felt tight. An aching pain made him gasp.

It's slipping away. I suddenly feel so old.

The lights. The crowd. The laughing, happy people.

It's all wrong. All wrong, Dierdre.

I've let this go on too long. And I know why, Robin decided. It's because I'm weak. I let myself fall for Dierdre. I didn't want her to die. I cared about her. I really did.

And because of her I let you down, Dad.

Because of her I let the park open. I didn't destroy it, burn it to the ground, blow it away.

As the lights flashed in his eyes, as the game booths tilted and swirled around him, Robin pictured his father. Nicholas Fear. So tall, so ramrod-straight, so stern.

Nicholas Fear would never have let this go on so long, Robin knew.

Nicholas Fear would have wiped the Bradley family—including Dierdre—off the face of the earth and then sat down to a good dinner.

But Robin was weak. Robin had feelings. Feelings that interfered with his promise to his father, his solemn vow to return the park land to the Fear family, its rightful owners.

I've failed you, Dad, Robin thought unhappily. The pain in his chest burned stronger. His legs felt weak and tired. Each wheezing breath made his lungs ache.

I've failed you—up till now.

I'm not an evil person, Robin told himself. Yes, I've done evil things. But only to keep my promise to you, Dad. But only to keep my vow to the Fear family, my family.

I've tried to be a good son, Dad. I've tried to do what you would do if you were here.

I've done evil things. But only to gain back what is rightfully ours. Everything I've done has been for the sake of justice.

Right, Dad? Right?

Sweat poured down Robin's forehead. Each breath sent a sharp pain to his chest.

I won't fail you, Dad, he vowed to himself. I promise. I've been weak. But I won't fail you now.

All of these thoughts raced through Robin's mind as he chased Dierdre down the brightly lit walk, darting between startled people, ducking around strollers and groups of kids.

He saw Dierdre stop, caught between a group of laughing teenagers and the side of a small food stand. With a final burst of energy, Robin dove for her.

He grabbed both shoulders and pinned her against the wall.

She stared at him, terror in her eyes. Her chest heaved as she gasped for breath. The red, blue, and yellow lights played over her frightened face.

No more talk, he decided. No more games. No more questions.

Well, actually, I have only one last question.

How shall I kill her?

chapter
24

Now what? Dierdre asked herself. Now what? Now what?

She let out a gasp as he pushed her back against the wall of the food stand.

I was stupid, she scolded herself. No way could I outrun him. Besides, where is there to run?

Wherever I ran in this park, he would find me.

She swallowed hard, her throat tight and dry. She sucked in breath after breath, thinking frantically, trying to decide how to save herself.

Raising her eyes to his, she forced out a shrill laugh. "Beat you!" she declared. She grinned at him, still breathing hard.

She saw his cold, dark eyes soften just a little. Saw a question on his face.

"You run like an old woman!" she teased.

His mouth dropped open. His eyes probed hers. "Do not!" he protested.

She forced another laugh. "Yes, you do."

You *are* old, she thought.

I know you are. I know the whole story, Robin.

But she didn't want to think about that now. She knew she was in danger. Real danger. She knew she had to find a way to get away from him. She had to stall him.

"That felt good," Dierdre said, brushing back her hair with both hands. "I've been cooped up all day. I just felt like running."

Is he buying it? she wondered.

Keep it light, she instructed herself. And just stall him. Stall him until Gary shows up.

He finally let go of her. He wiped sweat off his forehead with the palm of his hand.

"It wasn't a fair race," Robin complained. "You had too big a head start."

Dierdre glanced around, thinking hard. How do I stall him? How?

The sign on the front of the food stand caught her eye. "I'm suddenly so starving!" she exclaimed.

"Really?" His dark eyes still studied her uncertainly.

"How about some cotton candy?" she asked, starting toward the front of the stand. "I've been smelling it all night. It's hard to resist, isn't it?"

Robin hesitated. "Well . . ."

"Come on. Have some cotton candy. We'll share one," Dierdre urged, forcing herself to sound playful. Forcing herself to smile at him despite her fear. "My treat," she added.

"Uh . . . why don't you have one? I'll just take a taste," Robin replied.

They moved to the front of the stand. There was no line, so Dierdre stepped up and asked for a cone of cotton candy.

The young woman behind the counter moved to the cotton candy machine. She picked up a cone of white paper and began twirling it under the spinning pink sugar.

Dierdre watched the ball of cotton candy begin to form. Then she turned and searched the crowded walkway for Gary.

No sign of him. Did he forget?

Did something happen to him?

Robin eyed her warily. He stood close behind her, as if afraid she might turn and run again.

The young woman handed Dierdre the cone of cotton candy. The sweet aroma floated up to Dierdre. She reached for her wallet. "How much? A dollar?"

"No charge for you, Miss Bradley," the young woman replied.

Oh. That's right. I own this park, Dierdre remembered. She thanked her and lowered her face to the sticky pink candy.

She let the sweet taste slide down her tongue. Then she pulled off a hunk and pushed it into her mouth. It melted as soon as it hit her tongue.

Like magic, Dierdre thought. It's like spun magic. It just disappears when you touch it.

Beside her, Robin cleared his throat. She turned and saw him murmuring to himself, his face half hidden.

I wish I could touch him and make him disappear, Dierdre thought. I wish I could make him melt. Disappear forever.

Why was he suddenly talking to himself?

And where did this purple smoke come from? It appeared to swirl around them from the sides of the food stand.

Where's Gary? Taking another bite of the sticky pink sugar, Dierdre stepped away from the stand. Robin guided her back to the side wall.

She held out the cone to him. "Take a bite," she said forcing her voice to stay calm.

He ignored her. She saw his lips moving. Was he singing to himself?

"Robin, what are you doing?" she demanded. "I thought you wanted a taste."

She searched for Gary. Her heart skipped when she thought she saw him hurrying from the video game arcade toward her. But she quickly saw that it was another red-haired boy.

Not Gary . . .

What am I going to do? she wondered, feeling her muscles—all of her muscles—tighten in panic. I've got to keep stalling. Got to stall.

The purple smoke swirled thicker. It must be escaping from the Hatchet Show, Dierdre thought. They used a lot of purple smoke like this in the arena where the popular show was performed three times a night.

The thought of the kids in the show pretending to hatchet one another to bits made Dierdre shudder.

So much violence. So much violence on this land, on these acres that once were quiet, untouched woods.

And now she herself faced such danger—from this boy—this *old man*—this *Fear*.

She had to stall him. Had to pray that Gary would find her. Had to hope that Gary could somehow chase Robin off.

Dierdre shoved the cone playfully toward Robin's face. "Go on. Take a taste. It's strawberry. It's great."

Robin's hand shot up to push the cone away. The sticky pink ball of candy smashed into Dierdre's face.

Startled, she let out a cry. The sugar stuck to her cheeks. Her nose. "You creep!" she cried lightly, playfully.

She laughed.

I've got to pretend I'm having a good time, she thought. Got to stall him.

She stopped laughing when she felt the sticky pink stuff tighten over her face. "Hey!" She tried to cry out. But the candy spread over her mouth, gluing her lips together. "Hey—mmmmmph!"

What is happening? Dierdre wondered. She grabbed at the pink candy with both hands. But it stuck to her cheeks, her chin, her lips. She couldn't tug it off.

The purple smoke billowed up, forming a purple curtain around her, holding her inside its dark mists.

What is happening?

She clawed frantically, clawed with both hands at the cotton candy as it spread over her mouth, over her nose, over her eyes.

And as it spread, it tightened.

It squeezed her lips shut. And tightened over her nose. Growing heavier. Thicker.

"Help me!" she tried to scream. But the words came out in a groan, muffled beneath the thick, sticky goo.

Now she was tearing at it wildly. Tearing at the blanket of sticky pink candy. Tearing at her cheeks. Struggling to pull it off her nose.

She couldn't cry out. Couldn't open her mouth.

It pinched her face. Tightened around her chin.

She felt the sticky goo pushing into her nostrils.

She tried to blow out. Tried to pull it away from her nose.

But it covered her. Covered her. Covered her.

Sliding up her nose. Spreading stickily.

"I'll go get help!" she heard Robin cry.

She squinted into the purple fog. He had turned away from her and was running away.

"Don't move!" She couldn't see him. But she heard his voice. "Don't move, Dierdre! I'll get help!"

I—I can't breathe, Dierdre realized.

She dropped to her knees. Her hands still clawed desperately at the thick, sticky covering over her face.

It filled her nose. Covered her nostrils. Pressed in on her face. Pinched and spread and stuck.

Can't breathe . . .

Can't breathe . . .

chapter

25

"**I**'ll get help!" Robin called. He knew Dierdre couldn't see the broad smile on his face.

He ducked around the side of a game booth and crouched down, watching her struggle. Even through the swirls of purple fog, he could see her desperately grabbing at the mask of candy, clawing at her face, choking and gasping.

She dropped to her knees, frantically pulling at the thickening goo.

Robin's smile faded. "Goodbye, Dierdre," he murmured out loud.

In a few seconds she would be dead.

He tried to keep his mind clear. Tried to concentrate on the spell he had conjured.

But other thoughts, other pictures, forced their way into his mind.

He remembered her kisses. He remembered the

softness of her cheeks. He remembered the electric touch of her hands on his face.

The shock of conflicting emotions nearly burst him in two. His throat ached. His temples throbbed.

She has to die.

He knew she had to die. But he also wanted to keep her with him, to keep her alive.

He realized he was feeling many of the same emotions as sixty years ago—when he *had* to bring Meghan with him.

He cared about Meghan so much back then. He couldn't let her die with the other kids. He had to keep her alive with him—forever.

He wished he could do the same for Dierdre now. But of course he couldn't.

He had to let the cotton candy smother her. He had to finish what he had started.

He squinted through the purple fog. Dierdre was slumped on her knees. No longer clawing. No longer struggling.

No longer breathing, Robin was certain.

Waiting to die.

Robin held his breath. Waiting along with her. Watching.

Watching as a figure burst across the walk.

A familiar figure. Tall and lean. Bending down to Dierdre.

Gary?

Yes. Robin recognized him, even through the swirls of smoke.

What did he hold in his hand?

119

A large cup. Of soda? Of water?

"Nooo!" Robin let out a cry of protest. He jumped to his feet and plunged across the walkway.

Too late.

He saw Gary splash the drink on Dierdre's face.

Saw Dierdre's hands fly up. Saw her wiping away the thick layer of cotton candy.

The drink will melt it, Robin knew.

The spell will not hold under a splash of water.

The water will dissolve the mask of candy.

The purple smoke faded into the dark ground. Robin could see Dierdre clearly now. Could see the smile on her face. Could see the pink stains of candy on her cheeks as she took breath after breath.

Gary stood beside her, the empty drink cup still gripped in his hand.

Dierdre wiped more goo from her face. Brushed back her hair. And then she rushed forward with a joyful cry—and wrapped her arms around Gary.

His heart pounding, his temples pulsing, Robin froze, watching them hug.

No—this can't be happening. I was so close. So close. I don't believe this is happening.

I don't believe this boy has ruined things for me again.

Robin took a deep breath and made his way across the walk to them. "Dierdre—you're okay?" he cried.

She pulled away from Gary. The two of them stared at him, their expressions wary.

"I—I was so frightened!" Robin exclaimed. "Oh, thank goodness. I tried to get help. But I couldn't find anyone. I—"

He stopped and stared at Gary. Gary had his arm tightly wrapped around Dierdre's waist.

"Dierdre?" Robin cried, staring accusingly at Gary. "Who's this? Who *is* this?"

Dierdre hesitated. "Uh . . . well . . ."

Robin turned angrily to Gary. "Who are you?" he demanded.

chapter

26

Robin stepped up to Gary, challenging him. He saw a flash of fear in Gary's eyes.

Are they brave enough to tell me the truth? Robin wondered, staring Gary down.

I already know the truth about Gary. But are they brave enough to admit it? Or are you an eighty-year-old coward, Gary?

Gary opened his mouth to answer Robin's question. But Dierdre stepped between them and spoke first. "Uh . . . well . . . Robin . . ." She kept glancing tensely at Gary, standing in front of him as if protecting him.

"This is Gary," she said finally. "I've been meaning to tell you about Gary, Robin."

"Oh, really?" Robin replied, his eyes on Gary.

"You see," she started again, "Gary and I—we used to go together. I mean. Last year. But we sort of had a stupid fight. And we broke up."

"I see," Robin murmured.

"But now Gary is back," Dierdre continued. "And we sort of . . . well . . . got back together. I've been meaning to tell you about it, Robin. Really. I know you must think I've been acting weird lately. I—I—just didn't want to hurt you. See?"

Yes, I see, Robin thought bitterly.

I see that you're a total liar, Dierdre.

He turned his gaze from Gary to Dierdre, then back to Gary. Gary nodded his head, as if to say that he agreed with Dierdre.

You're both liars, Robin thought, feeling the rage build inside him.

"I see," he muttered to Dierdre. He lowered his eyes, pretending to be hurt. "I thought that you and I . . ." He let his voice trail off sadly.

"I didn't want to hurt you," Dierdre repeated. "But Gary and I—we . . . well . . . we've known each other for a long time."

Liar!

Robin wanted to spit the word in her face.

Do you think I'm stupid, Dierdre? Do you think I could live eighty years and be as stupid as that?

Don't you think I'm smart enough to figure out the truth?

You and Gary didn't go together last year. Because Gary is as old as I am. Gary comes from the 1930s too. Gary is here to ruin my plans. You've been acting weird, Dierdre, because Gary told you all about me.

But the two of you are too afraid to tell the truth.

And you've got reason to be.

"I see," Robin said softly, doing his best to act

123

disappointed and upset. "Well, I'm glad you're okay. When you started to choke, I guess I panicked. I'm really sorry."

"That's okay," Dierdre replied, glancing at Gary. He still had his arm wrapped around her waist.

"Well . . . see you later," Robin said. He gave her a shrug, as if to signal that he was too upset to say more. Then he turned and headed slowly toward the front gate.

I know you're an immortal, Gary, Robin thought. But there must be a way that immortals can be killed. And I plan to find that way tonight.

And once you're no longer around to protect Dierdre, it will be easy to kill her too. And close Fear Park down for good.

The thought of going into his library and browsing through the old books to find a spell to kill Gary cheered Robin up. He had a smile on his face all the way home.

Robin planned to stay up all night, reading through the ancient books in his library. But to his surprise, he found the spell he was looking for in the very first book.

A stack of dusty books had been left on the table. Robin had picked up the book on top of the stack.

And near the back he had found the spell. According to the book, this was the only known spell to end the life of someone who had been made immortal.

Robin stared at the spell in shock. What luck! he thought. To find what I'm looking for so easily.

His eyes drifted over the page. He squinted to read the tiny type on the cracked and yellowed paper.

He stopped at a paragraph near the beginning and read the words twice, carefully making sure he understood. It told him that an immortal cannot be killed by anyone living. An immortal can be killed only by the dead.

And the dead person must be someone the immortal knew.

Someone the immortal knows . . .

Who did Gary know back in 1935? Robin wondered.

He closed his eyes and thought hard. After a while he knew what he had to do.

I will bring back all the kids who died hatcheting one another to death. At least one of them had to know Gary.

I don't remember any of their names. It's been so many years.

But I can bring them all back. Back from the dead.

And using this spell, I can instruct them to kill Gary. To bring Gary back to the world of the dead with them.

Robin read the spell carefully. Then he read it again, thinking hard. Thinking about how to make it work.

Bringing so many kids back from the dead was risky.

Would he be able to control them? Would they obey him and kill Gary?

According to the book, he could control them

easily. The spell gave him the words that made him their master.

Leaning over the big book, Robin whispered the words, practicing them, rehearsing them. It was a difficult spell. It required a lot of skill.

As Robin whispered the words, learning to pronounce each one, he heard a shuffling at the library door. Then a muffled cough.

I know you're there, Meghan, he thought. Raising his eyes to the door, he saw her shadow lean across the floor.

I know you're outside the door, spying on me.

But don't worry, my dear Meghan. I haven't forgotten you.

I have plans for you too.

He set the trap for Meghan at breakfast the next morning.

"You know, I think I've been neglecting you," Robin said, pouring himself a cup of coffee.

"Yes, you have," Meghan replied softly. She wore a blue robe over her pajamas. Her face was still creased from sleep. Tangles of red hair fell over the shoulders of the robe.

She set down her coffee cup and stared intently across the table at him, waiting for him to continue.

"I think you should get out more," Robin continued. He stirred a teaspoon of sugar into the steaming coffee. "Why don't you meet me at the park tonight."

Her mouth opened in a small O of surprise. "At the park?"

Robin nodded. "I want to show you something. I

think you'll find it interesting." He continued to stir the coffee, his dark eyes locked on hers. "Meet me at the Hatchet Show."

"Huh? The show?" Her voice was still hoarse from sleep. She made a disgusted face. "Robin—you know I hate that show."

"I know," Robin started. "But tonight—"

"It brings back so many horrible memories," Meghan continued, lowering her eyes to her coffee cup. She rubbed at a stain on the red-checkered tablecloth.

"Meghan, it happened over sixty years ago," Robin scolded. "An entire lifetime ago."

"I know that," she replied sharply. "But to me it seems like yesterday." She sighed and brushed a strand of hair off her face. "You should understand that, Robin. You should understand that by now."

"I do," he protested. "But—"

"Those kids were my friends. I knew most of them for my whole life. And I stood there, stood there in the woods and watched my friends go into a frenzy. I watched them hack and chop one another to bits. I—I'll never forget the sight of the blood soaking the ground. So much blood. The ground was red, Robin. Red! All this time, and I can't get that picture out of my mind."

"I know," Robin said softly. He stood up, crossed to her side of the table, and tenderly placed his hand on her shoulder. "I know."

"It just makes me sick that they act out that scene every night in the park," Meghan continued, shaking her head. "For entertainment. For entertainment."

She turned her face to him, her expression accusing. "Your father cast that spell—didn't he? Your father made those kids murder one another—right? We've never talked about it. All these years, and I never wanted to ask you. But it's true, isn't it, Robin?"

Robin swallowed hard. He nodded solemnly. "Yes, it's true," he lied.

Robin knew very well that he himself had cast the spell. But he would never confess that to Meghan. No need. Meghan wasn't going to exist after tonight.

"And that's why you feel so guilty," Meghan said, taking his hand from her shoulder and pressing it gently between her hands. "That's why you've worked so hard to protect the Bradleys. That's why you've worked so hard to protect them against your father's curse—isn't it, Robin?"

"Yes," he told her. "That's the truth."

He wanted to laugh out loud. Laugh in her face.

How could she have lived with him for sixty years and never guessed the truth?

"Will you meet me tonight?" he asked in a whisper, leaning over her, his lips brushing her ear. "Will you meet me at the show tonight? I really want to show you something. I really think you will want to see it."

She thought about it for a long while. Then she finally replied with a whispered "Okay."

A smile spread across Robin's face.

One down and two to go, he thought happily.

Now if I can get Dierdre and Gary to join us there, it will be an unforgettable night—for everyone!

chapter
27

Robin knocked on the trailer door. Then, without waiting for a reply, pulled the door open and stepped inside.

The afternoon sun beamed down brightly. The trailer felt steamy inside, the air hot and stale. Robin blinked, waiting for his eyes to adjust to the dim light, and saw Dierdre turn from her father's desk.

She wore a sleeveless blue T-shirt over white tennis shorts. Her brown hair was pulled back, a ponytail at the side held in place with a blue hair scrunchie.

"Robin?" She didn't hide her surprise at seeing him.

"I just came to see how you are," he said. "You're okay?"

She nodded. "Yes. Fine."

"I mean, that was so scary last night," he added innocently. "When you started to choke . . ."

"I'm never eating cotton candy again," Dierdre

groaned. "It was weird. It clung to my face and wouldn't come off. I really thought I'd suffocate."

"I'm so glad you're okay," Robin lied, pleased with how sincere he sounded.

"Nice of you to stop by," she said stiffly. She turned to the papers on the cluttered desk. "I really can't talk now. I have to work."

"I'll get going," Robin replied. "I just wanted to say . . . uh . . . no hard feelings."

She narrowed her eyes at him. "Excuse me?"

"About Gary, I mean," Robin said, lowering his gaze to the floor.

"Oh. Right," Dierdre replied awkwardly. He heard the coldness slip back into her voice.

"I hope we can still be friends," Robin said softly.

Dierdre muttered a reply. He couldn't hear what she said.

"How long have you known Gary?" he asked. He wanted to see her squirm, wanted to force her to think fast.

"Since grade school," she replied quickly.

Liar, he thought, not changing his expression.

There are two liars in this trailer right now, Dierdre, Robin wanted to say. Tomorrow, one of us will be dead.

Tomorrow this trailer will have a padlock on it. In fact, the whole park will have a padlock on it. And a sign that reads CLOSED FOREVER.

He started to the door. Then stopped and turned back to her. "Do me a favor?"

She frowned. "I don't know . . ."

"Meet me tonight? At the Hatchet Show? The eight o'clock show?"

"Huh? Are you serious?"

"I want you to see something," Robin said eagerly. "You'll be amazed. Really. And bring Gary."

"Gary?"

He could see the confusion on her face. Confusion mixed with curiosity.

"Just come," he urged, flashing her his best smile. "You and Gary. To the eight o'clock show. It's the last favor I'll ever ask you. I promise."

Dierdre and Gary arrived at the outdoor theater at ten to eight. Dierdre led him to a seat in the front row.

"Why are we doing this?" Gary demanded.

Dierdre squeezed his hand. "I already told you," she replied impatiently. "Robin wants to show us something."

"But he isn't even here," Gary protested, glancing to the entrance.

"Just wait," Dierdre instructed.

She cast her eyes around the small theater. It was nearly empty, she saw. A group of teenagers huddled together in the top row. There were maybe twenty or thirty other people scattered around the rest of the theater.

Low clouds overhead blocked the moon and threatened rain. In the far distance she could see jagged streaks of pale lightning flickering in the clouds.

The threatening weather had kept people home. The entire park was nearly deserted.

Dierdre's stomach felt fluttery. Her hands were cold and wet. She stuffed them into the pockets of her shorts and slumped low in the seat beside Gary.

Let's get this over with, she thought nervously.

Band music from the 1930s blared from the loud-speakers overhead. Purple spotlights beamed over the rows of tree stumps that dotted the ground.

Soon the actors would come out, she knew. Teenagers dressed in clothes from the 1930s. They would talk and laugh, and then set to work, chopping at the tree stumps with their axes, clearing the ground for Fear Park.

And then the music would swell, and the eerie purple smoke would swirl over the theater. And the teenage work crew would go into its frenzy, hacking and chopping at one another. Chopping off arms and legs. Lopping off heads. Spilling the fake blood over the ground. Horrifying the audience, giving everyone the sick thrills they all came to see.

Dierdre craned her neck and gazed toward the theater entrance. Where was Robin?

She glanced at her watch. Five to eight.

Where was he?

"This is dumb," Gary complained. His eyes were on the thickening storm clouds so low overhead. "It's going to rain. We're going to get drenched."

"Just relax," Dierdre pleaded. "Robin wanted to show us—"

She stopped when she saw Robin enter the theater. His eyes moved along the mostly empty seats until he spotted Gary and her. He smiled and guided his friend toward them, waving to Dierdre.

"This is Meghan," he said breathlessly. "Meghan, this is Gary and Dierdre."

"Robin has told me a lot about you," Meghan said awkwardly to Dierdre. She sat down next to Dierdre. Still smiling, Robin lowered himself to the seat at the end of the row.

He certainly seems excited, Dierdre told herself, studying Robin. He's practically ready to burst!

She leaned across Meghan to talk to Robin. "Why did you make us come here?" she demanded.

Robin's smile grew wider. "You'll see."

"This show is so sick," Gary commented.

Robin laughed loudly, as if Gary had cracked a really funny joke.

I've never seen Robin so *psyched!* Dierdre thought. He keeps staring from Gary to me to Meghan, and his smile gets wider and wider.

"Its sad, really," Meghan said seriously.

"It's sad that people love watching this kind of thing," Gary agreed.

Dierdre didn't say anything. Watching Robin's gleeful excitement, she suddenly felt sick. She swallowed hard, struggling to keep her dinner down. Her cold hands shoved deep in her pockets, she took a deep breath and held it.

The lights dimmed. The music boomed louder.

Dierdre shut her eyes as the purple smoke floated up from the ground. She swallowed again. Her mouth felt dry as cotton.

When she opened her eyes, the actors were making

their way through the billowing smoke onto the field of tree stumps. The field stretched in darkness. The performers were shadowy figures, moving in twos and threes, axes on their shoulders.

Dierdre turned to glance at her companions. Gary was slumped deep in his seat, his knees on the low concrete wall in front of them. Meghan sat tensely, her back straight, her hands folded tightly in her lap.

Robin leaned forward eagerly, smiling, excited. His lips were moving rapidly, Dierdre saw. As if he were singing or talking to himself.

Thick clouds of purple smoke floated over the theater. The music throbbed. The sound vibrated off the concrete walls and the empty seats.

The teenage workers were still hidden in darkness. They moved slowly together, murmuring, laughing quietly. A few of them took practice swings with their axes.

Dierdre sighed, eager for the lights to come up and the performance to start. She felt a cold shiver run down her back.

She turned once again to Robin. He leaned practically into the field area. He had his elbows on the low concrete wall. His head propped in his hands.

His face was half hidden by his hands. But she could see his lips moving, see the tight look of concentration on his face.

Dierdre forced herself to turn back to the field. The overhead spotlights brightened, cutting through the swirls of smoke.

The music grew softer.

The lights grew brighter. Brighter. Bright as day.

And then the teenage workers all turned. All turned at once to face the audience.

Dierdre gasped.

She heard loud gasps and cries all around.

She saw Gary's mouth drop open and his eyes bulge.

She saw Meghan raise her hands to her head and tug at her hair, her features twisted in shock.

And then, staring at the faces . . . the faces . . . the hideous faces on the field . . . Gary, Meghan, Dierdre—they *all* began to scream in horror.

chapter

29

"They're not actors!" Dierdre heard herself scream. "They're not actors!"

Gary let out a cry of pain.

Dierdre glanced down. Saw that she was squeezing his arm. Squeezing it so hard. It took real effort to let go.

"Nooooo! Noooooo!" Beside her, Meghan tugged at the sides of her hair and moaned in horror.

The teenagers on the field staggered and lurched toward the seats. Dragging themselves into the light. The bright lights. So bright Dierdre could see every detail of their decaying faces.

She could see the rotting green skin. The dark, empty scockets that had once held eyes.

She could see the worms curling out of the open nostrils. The swarms of bugs crawling from the holes where the ears had been.

The matted hair. The gaping rips and holes in the scalp where gray bone poked through.

And the smell!

The foul, putrid, sour smell. The smell of dead, rotting meat. Of insects and decay . . .

Clutching Gary again, trembling in fear, trembling, every muscle quivering, her jaw bouncing, out of control . . . out of control . . . gasping . . . gasping for breath . . . Dierdre stared as the teenagers staggered closer.

"They're not actors! They're not actors!" She couldn't stop shrieking the words. She couldn't let go of Gary.

They're dead, Dierdre knew.

They're really dead.

They look dead. They smell dead. They move so stiffly, so painfully, as if they haven't moved in sixty years!

The dead figures dragged themselves across the field, moving in a ragged line. Side by side.

An arm fell off a boy's shoulder and bounced heavily on the ground.

Worms dropped from a girl's nose and ears as she moved closer. The flesh of one leg had rotted away, the exposed bones creaking as she hobbled.

A head fell off. It landed on its jaw near a tree stump. The body kept moving, dragging itself on with slow, painful, shuffling steps.

Closer, they staggered.

Gary jumped to his feet. Dierdre could see his legs shaking. He stood unsteadily, but didn't try to walk away or run.

Frozen in horror. Gary is frozen in horror, Dierdre realized.

Holding her breath, trying to shut out the putrid odor, Dierdre turned to Robin. He hadn't moved. He leaned toward the approaching dead, his lips moving rapidly, chanting, chanting, his face open with excitement. So thrilled.

Closer they came. Dragging themselves. Staggering. Some of them headless or armless, crawling now.

And then Dierdre saw Meghan open her mouth in a shriek of terror.

"They—they're coming for us!" Meghan cried. "They're coming for *us!*"

chapter 30

Fingerless hands reached out toward them.

Rotted heads rolled on shoulders. Toothless mouths opened in ugly groans. Bugs crawled down chins and in the empty eye sockets.

"They're coming for us!" Meghan wailed. "For us!"

Dierdre sucked in a mouthful of sour air and held it. She struggled to stop trembling, to stop her muscles from quivering, her whole body from shaking.

The dead figures reached out. Leaned over the low concrete wall. Reached out with their green, rotted hands.

Turned with low groans from deep inside their hollow chests.

Turned.

And grabbed Robin.

Grabbed him. Pulled him. Tugged Robin over the wall.

Robin's hands shot up. Dierdre saw his eyes bulge wide.

"Hey!" was all he managed to cry.

And then he was down on his elbows and knees on the grass.

The dead kids pulled him down and held him, grinning toothless grins, gaping holes where lips had once been.

They held him down. And Dierdre saw the axes raised.

Saw the axes raised so slowly, so painfully.

And then the axes began to swing down.

The dead kids took turns. They brought the axes down one at a time.

The first swing sliced off Robin's head.

The next dead teenager chopped deeply into Robin's back.

Another swing cut off Robin's right arm.

Robin's body twitched and shuddered.

The blades fell. Again. Again.

Again again again.

A singing, whistling sound. Followed each time by a solid *thunk*.

They didn't stop their silent, steady work until they had chopped Robin to tiny bits of meat and bone.

And then a joyous roar rang out from somewhere inside the dead, empty bodies.

And Dierdre and Meghan jumped up. And Meghan threw her arms around Dierdre. And cried: "Thank you! Thank you, Dierdre, for helping to set me free—at last!"

chapter 31

Dierdre hugged Meghan back. Held on to her. Tears ran down their cheeks.

"Thank you. Thank you," Meghan repeated in a choked whisper. "I couldn't have done it without you, Dierdre."

"No—please—" Dierdre protested. "Thank *you*, Meghan. For warning me about Robin. For coming to me and telling me the truth about him."

"He thought I didn't know," Meghan said, letting her tears flow. "He thought he had me fooled. I trusted Robin for so long. But when I found out the truth, I had to pay him back—for what he did to me and to all my friends."

"Meghan, thank you! You've ended the curse. You've ended Robin's hold on all of us. We're both free now. Both free!"

"Goodbye, Dierdre!" Meghan called. She leapt

over the wall to join her friends, her friends of so long ago.

Dierdre watched as they went howling from the theater. Then, leaning on Gary, she followed them out. Out into the fresh-smelling air. Away from the horror and the rancid odor of death.

She saw the dead kids moving over the park. Climbing onto the rides. Shrieking and howling in wild joy.

They finally got their free admission, Dierdre realized.

They finally got to enjoy the park.

The purple smoke billowed thickly, surrounding her, surrounding everything, a thick curtain of fog. She could hear their squeals and howls of delight. She could hear them on the Inferno roller coaster. Shrill shrieks, shrieks of the dead come to life, shrieks that grew to a deafening howl.

And then silence.

The purple smoke faded to wisps along the ground.

Gone, Dierdre saw. The dead kids were all gone.

Meghan too, she knew.

Poor Meghan.

All gone now. The park silent and empty.

After sixty years, they had their brief time in the park. And now they were gone.

Gary grabbed both of her hands. He pulled her close.

I forgot all about him! Dierdre realized.

She saw the fear lingering in his eyes. "What happened?" he whispered. "Dierdre—I don't understand."

"We defeated the Fears," Dierdre sighed. "Meghan and I—we defeated the Fears and the curse they put on the park."

She pressed her forehead against Gary's shoulder. She just wanted him to hold her, hold her, hold her safe forever.

"Meghan came to me," Dierdre explained. "After Robin pushed Daddy into the Ferris wheel. Meghan saw the whole thing. She knew then that Robin had lied to her, lied to her for sixty years."

Dierdre wrapped her arms around Gary's waist. She held on tightly to him, as if he might disappear along with the others.

"So Meghan came to me and told me the whole story," she continued breathlessly. "She took me to their house. We read through Robin's books of evil spells. Meghan and I practiced them and practiced them. We had to destroy him. We knew if we worked together, we could.

"We found the spell to bring back the dead," Dierdre told Gary. "And then we made our plan. Meghan picked a fight with Robin to make sure he was angry enough to want to destroy her. Then we left the book with the spell on top of his stack, where he would find it easily."

She squeezed Gary's hand. Held him close. "We made Robin think that you came from the past. We made him think that you were an immortal too, come here to destroy him."

Gary's mouth dropped open. "Who? Me?" he cried. "An immortal? Me?"

"Meghan and I didn't want him to know that we

were working together. So we told him you were a kid from the 1930s. We made him suspect you."

Gary shook his head. "I don't believe this!" he declared.

"I believe it," Dierdre said, holding on to him. "I believe it. Meghan and I worked so long and hard on our secret plan. Tonight Robin thought that he was calling up the dead. He thought *he* called those poor kids up from the grave.

"But Meghan and I did it. We did it earlier. We did it first. We did it and we sent them against Robin. They got their revenge. And now he is gone. And his evil is gone. The curse is gone. I know Daddy will be okay now that the curse is lifted."

She raised her face to Gary's. "And we'll be okay too. I know we will."

Holding on to him, she began guiding him to the front gate, walking slowly, feeling him beside her, breathing the cool fresh air, listening to the clear, crisp silence.

The silence . . .

What *was* that soft sound behind them as they walked?

Was it the whisper of voices thankfully, peacefully, returned to their graves?

Or the echo of the calliope—soft, happy music from the carousel?

were working together. So we told him you were a kid
of 9 in the 1970s. We made him suspect you."

Gary shook his head. "I don't believe this," he
muttered.

"I believe it," Deedre said, holding on to him. "I
believe it, Meghan, and it worked so long and hard on
our secret plan. Tonight Kevin thought that he was
calling up the dead. He thought he raised those poor
kids up from the grave."

"But Meghan and I did it. We'd it earlier. We did
it first. We dug it and we saw them against Robin.
They got him enraged. And now he is gone. And his
evil is gone. The curse is gone. I know Daddy will be
okay now that the curse is lifted."

She raised her face to Gary's. "And we'll be okay
too, I know we will."

Holding on to him, she began guiding him to the
front gate, walking slowly, feeling him become happy,
becoming the cool fresh air, fragrant in the clear,
crisp silence.

"The suspects —"

Was that the soft sound behind them, as they
walked?

Will it the whisper of voices thankfully, peacefully
returned to their graves?

Or the echo of the rattles — soft, happy rattles
from the grave?

About the Author

"Where do you get your ideas?"

That's the question that R. L. Stine is asked most often. "I don't know where my ideas come from," he says. "But I do know that I have a lot more scary stories in my mind that I can't wait to write."

So far, he has written nearly five dozen mysteries and thrillers for young people, all of them bestsellers.

Bob grew up in Columbus, Ohio. Today he lives in an apartment near Central Park in New York City with his wife, Jane, and son, Matt.

THE NIGHTMARES
NEVER END . . .
WHEN YOU VISIT

Next . . .
NIGHT GAMES
(Coming mid-October 1996)

Diana and her friends thought they would never see Spencer Jarvis again. He moved away from Shadyside a year ago.

Now he's back. And he wants Diana and the others to go out with him late at night, when the whole town is asleep. He convinces them to play his night games—dangerous practical jokes on other people in the neighborhood.

At first Diana thinks it's exciting to sneak out after midnight, never knowing what Spencer will have planned. But the jokes grow more and more menacing. Until someone ends up dead.